TAU CETI

TAU CETI

KEVIN J. ANDERSON

SEQUEL NOVELETTE BY
STEVEN SAVILE

THE STELLAR GUILD SERIES
TEAM-UPS WITH BESTSELLING AUTHORS

MIKE RESNICK
SERIES EDITOR

an imprint of

Rockville, Maryland

ISBN: 978-1-61242-047-9

www.PhoenixPick.com
Great Science Fiction & Fantasy
Free Ebook every month

Published by Phoenix Pick
an imprint of Arc Manor
P. O. Box 10339
Rockville, MD 20849-0339
www.ArcManor.com

CONTENTS

A GREETING FROM THE SERIES EDITOR

HELLO, AND WELCOME to *The Stellar Guild*, a new series by Phoenix Pick, the science fiction imprint of Arc Manor. I'm Mike Resnick, the series editor.

Over the years I've worked with a number of beginning writers. Hugo winner Maureen McHugh refers to them as "Mike's Writer Children". The reason I (and others) do this is quite simple: in the field of science fiction, almost every writer who helped today's stars and journeymen is either rich, dead, or both, and since it is impractical to pay them back by the time we're in a position to, we pay forward. I have worked with eight writers who went on to be Campbell nominees (the Campbell is science fiction's Rookie-of-the-Year award), as well as some whose success came later or occasionally not at all.

The thing is, I'm not unique. Just about every writer I know pays forward in much the same way in this most generous of literary fields, and when Arc Manor publisher Shahid Mahmud was looking for a new line that featured a new approach, we put our heads together and hit upon what has become *The Stellar Guild*, in which each book features, not a collaboration, but a team-up between a superstar of our field, who will write an original novella, and a protégé of the superstar's own choosing, who will write a novelette set in the same universe.

You know what I love about this field? When I first approached each of our superstars—Kevin J. Anderson,

Mercedes Lackey, Eric Flint, all the rest—and said I was editing a new line and wanted a novella, and we would pay such-and-so for it, everyone politely declined. After all, their services are in great demand, they're contracted years ahead, and Arc Manor was offering substantial-but-not-Wall-Street pay rates.

But the second I explained that I also wanted a novelette in the same book, with full credit on the front cover, from a protégé of their choosing, every last one of them instantly changed course and agreed to write for *The Stellar Guild*.

Some of the protégés, like Steve Savile, have already sold a few books and had some success; others are virtually unsold prior to their *Stellar Guild* appearance. What they have in common, besides talent, is that each of them has a friend and role model who's helping them up the ladder.

So here you have it—a brand new line, in which today's superstars strut their literary stuff, and also introduce you to the early work of the next generation of Hugo winners and bestsellers.

Mike Resnick

TAU CETI

Book One
TORTOISE AND HARE

KEVIN J. ANDERSON

PART ONE

1

196 years since the Beacon's *departure from Earth.*
21 years to scheduled arrival at Tau Ceti.

BURTON PELLAR, THE NINTH CAPTAIN of the generation ship *Beacon*, was dead, and more than two decades remained before the starship was due to arrive at Tau Ceti.

The *Beacon's* thousands of crewmember-colonists gathered in mess halls, community chambers, and exercise domes, getting close to any public transmission screen that would show the funeral ceremony taking place down in the main cargo bay.

Though she was only fourteen, Jorie Taylor was one of the privileged few invited to attend the ceremonies in person. Kora Andropolis, in line to be the *Beacon's* tenth Captain, had taken a liking to the girl and asked her to be present.

Dressed in their best shipclothes, Jorie's parents joined her for Captain Pellar's memorial. Everyone remained quiet as a string quartet played "Spring" from Vivaldi's "Four Seasons," which had been the Captain's favorite piece. During the slowship's two-century-long voyage, the people aboard—descendants of the original pioneers—had taken care to preserve and revere the cultural masterpieces from their homeworld. The crewmember-colonists knew where they were going, as well as where they had been and who they were.

Beside her, Jorie's twelve-year-old brother fidgeted, and she nudged him to be still; Steven didn't see the historical significance of what they were witnessing. For both of them, Pellar was the only Captain they had ever known; he had assumed the role the very year her brother was born, when Jorie was only two. Very little changed aboard the *Beacon* as it toiled across empty space, but this was a dramatic shift.

Jorie knew her ship's history and had studied the Captains. The first, Delda Rochelle, took the slowship's helm when it was finally completed after many decades of construction; Captain Rochelle guided the *Beacon* under gradual but constant acceleration away from the turmoil of a seemingly dying planet, leaving Earth and the Moon behind. It took them twenty years just to leave the home solar system.

And after that a journey of 11.9 light years lay ahead of them before they reached Tau Ceti and what they hoped was a habitable planet: Sarbras.

The ship's second Captain, Templesmith, had served for twenty-five years, overseeing the difficult but subtle transition as the group of hopeful pioneers leaving Earth became a generation of voyagers. They spent their entire lives in transit, knowing that not even their great-great-grandchildren would survive to see the *Beacon* arrive at its destination. Then came Captains Blake, Wexler, Chan, Marius, Orov, Ramirez, and Captain Pellar.

Most of the leaders in the middle of the voyage were unremarkable, unmemorable, Jorie thought. They served through a century and a half of complacency, even malaise (except for the power-failure disaster in year 118). Those past Captains were little more than names in the history texts, like a list of colony equipment, an inventory of prefab shelters, or the catalog of plant seeds and animal embryos stored in deep-freeze ready to be reawakened once the ship arrived.

Twenty-one more years.

For the first time, she realized—truly *felt* it in her gut—that she and her brother would be part of the first generation to see the fruition of so many dreams. They were going to set foot on a virgin world and make it humanity's second home.

Their home.

When the string quartet finished, followed by an awkward smattering of applause, Kora Andropolis stepped up to the plastic-wrapped cocoon that held the Captain's body. Burton Pellar rested on a rectangular supply crate, which had been draped with a blue cloth so that it looked like an altar.

"Captain Pellar brought us this far." The compact, middle-aged woman had short brown hair that was lightly salted with gray strands. Andropolis was generally soft-spoken, though she did not suffer fools. Fortunately, she did not consider Jorie a fool.

"For ten years, he guided this ship, and brought us a full light year closer to Tau Ceti. Now, the *Beacon* has to go on without him—and, yes, we will go on. As your new Captain, I'll do my best to see that we arrive safely at our destination."

Burton Pellar hadn't been a warm man and kept himself distant from the crew, but he had not been disliked. The years of his Captaincy had passed without drama, disaster, or political turmoil. Jorie supposed that most Captains would consider *uneventful* decades a sign of success.

"Burton Pellar was my friend," Andropolis continued. "We will honor and remember him. I'm sure we can find a continent or a mountain range on Sarbras to name after him." She gave a small smile in an attempt to lighten the mood. "Now we set him free to drift among the stars with the other Captains, as a waypoint on our journey."

She stepped back from the wrapped body. Council members who'd been appointed pallbearers came forward, picked up the Captain, and carried him over to a small maintenance airlock chamber.

Jorie's parents stared straight ahead. Steven was at last interested. When an average colonist died, his or her body was reclaimed, processed, and recycled to fertilize the vegetation in the greenhouse dome. But Captains were special—they were set free.

After Andropolis activated the inner hatch of the airlock, the four pallbearers placed the shrouded body inside the chamber. They sealed the hatch again, and the head of life-support punched the controls. "Goodbye, Burton," he whispered.

During the airlock-cycling process, Jorie looked around the cargo bay's sealed crates that had been stacked there almost two centuries earlier: excavating machinery, mining equipment, prefabricated shelters, tools, ready-made satellites to be deployed around their new planet. Experts and precision engineers regularly inventoried, checked, and maintained the equipment, but there was little to do with it but wait while the ship crossed space.

Finally, the last breaths of air slipped out of the airlock chamber; when the outer hatch opened, the pressure differential was enough to nudge the wrapped body. Burton Pellar eased out into the starry vacuum, separating from the *Beacon* on his own journey.

Getting down to business, the Noah—a smiling and avuncular, silver-haired man (who had no other name as far as Jorie knew; his position was all that mattered)—turned to Andropolis. He looked like some druidic forest wizard. "Change is a constant in the cycle of life. It is with great pleasure, and continued hope, that I now appoint Kora Andropolis as the *Beacon*'s tenth Captain." He pinned a symbolic star on the lapel of the clean, white jacket she had donned for the ceremony. "See us safely on our way, Captain."

That ended the formal part of the ceremony, and the gathering quickly devolved into casual conversation and continued congratulations. Jorie felt proud for her mentor, and her parents worked their way through the crowd to shake the new Captain's hand, and they made Steven do the same, so that he would remember it.

When Jorie's turn came, she said, "I'll always remember this, Captain." The word sounded strange in her mouth. *Captain*. Still caught up in pondering the *Beacon*'s long voyage, she added, "You might be our last one. Isn't that exciting?"

Andropolis gave her a warm smile. "If I'm optimistic, yes, I might live long enough to see our ship to Sarbras, but by no means will I be the *last* Captain. Our mission doesn't end once we arrive at the planet—it's just the beginning. There's more to a long journey than just getting to the finish line."

Jorie bit her lip, thinking of all the increased responsibilities that Andropolis now shouldered. Seeing her concern, the older woman smiled and placed a hand on her shoulder. "Captain Pellar trained me very well. He prepared me for everything I needed to know." She gave a firm squeeze. "I only hope I can do the same for you."

Jorie wasn't sure she understood. "What do you mean, Captain?"

"We should start as soon as possible. I'm taking you on as my protégée to prepare you for your role as the *Beacon*'s eleventh Captain...whenever it's time."

2

INSIDE THE FENCED COMPOUND of Complex Alpha, Earth's largest government space-research facility, Andre Pellar watched the transmission that had just arrived from the ancient slowship *Beacon*. He kept the sound low and hunched above the screen in an attempt to hide what he was doing; he would be in trouble if anyone caught him wasting time on irrelevant matters when he was supposed to focus his concentration on the job at hand.

Though his defense likely wouldn't hold water, Andre considered the message part of his work; the progress, and fate, of the enormous generation ship was certainly relevant to their massive project. He hoped the chief scientist would back him up, but that depended on what kind of mood Dr. Max Chambers-Osawa was in.

Even if he suffered a revocation of privileges or a reduction in food rations, he doubted the consequences would be overly severe. Andre was a talented theoretical physicist, second only to Dr. Max. The project needed him.

Most of the research conducted behind the security fences was defense-related—weapon designs and surveillance-and-security systems to crack down on unrest. But President Jurudu had a soft spot for Dr. Max's pie-in-the-sky project, though it was a long-term study and might not bear fruit for a dozen or more years. The President continued the funding and allowed them some leeway.

The *Beacon* still had more than two decades before its arrival at Tau Ceti, provided the slowship was on course and on schedule after two centuries in flight.

Even after so much time had passed, the colony vessel continued to broadcast annual updates. The thousands aboard assumed that those who were still struggling on Earth would cheer them on (and Andre quietly *did*, although he was in the minority).

Most people, however, no longer paid much attention to the long-gone colony vessel. Due to the distance and transmission delay, by the time the *Beacon*'s news reached Earth, it was more than a decade out of date. The slowship's concerns and triumphs were too distant to have any relevance in their daily struggle. How could a vessel that was ten light years away, and which had nearly bankrupted Earth in the midst of catastrophic ecological ruin, matter to them at all anymore? In his quest to find a scapegoat for propaganda purposes, President Jurudu fostered public resentment against the *Beacon*, and they were much too far away to defend themselves.

Andre (privately) believed that the generation ship carried humanity's Plan B, their second chance. The annual transmission, which Earth had just received via long-distance high-intensity packet, was particularly meaningful to him. Though the news was ten years old, the *Beacon* announced the recommendation and selection of Burton Pellar as their new Captain. Andre had never met the man, but he knew that the Pellars aboard the slowship were his distant cousins. His own ancestors were from another branch of the family that had stayed behind; nevertheless, he still felt a connection to them.

Dr. Max cleared his throat, startling Andre. "That man's rather old to be chosen as Captain, don't you think?"

Feeling guilty, Andre fumbled with the screen, but it was too late to blank the file. Instead of scolding the young man for watching the message packet, Dr. Max wore an amused and superior smile. His shoulder-length salt-and-pepper hair looked windblown. "He won't last to the end of the voyage."

Life expectancy on Earth had shortened because of environmental hazards, austerity measures, and contaminants, especially in recent years. Even so, Andre didn't think Captain Pellar looked particularly old, perhaps in his sixties. "It's conceivable he could live another few decades, sir."

Dr. Max always had a condescending attitude toward the colonists. "He might be dead already, with all the radiation they're exposed to in deep space. Remember, the *Beacon*'s technology is two hundred years out of date. Who knows what medical techniques their doctors practice? Leeches? Bleeding?"

Andre knew better than to argue with the blustery physicist, choosing not to point out that the medical technology available when the slowship departed was actually superior to what the frayed Earth possessed at present.

More than two centuries ago, the sun had entered a violent cycle of solar flares, which caused significant damage to the ozone layer and the environment. With climate collapse causing one catastrophe after another, and cancer running rampant among the population, the nations of Earth had made a gigantic last-ditch effort.

The highest-resolution scans from orbiting telescopes and long-range probes found an Earth-sized planet in the habitable zone around Tau Ceti, nearly twelve light-years away. Out of hope and desperation grew a the germ of a project that required what humanity had never been good at—long-range planning.

The idea was initiated by wealthy, private visionaries who funded an escape ship, at first. But, as the project grew and word spread, other governments signed on, culminating in the construction of the enormous generation ship, a project on a breathtaking scale that had never been matched in history.

Building the *Beacon* took twenty turbulent years. Long-range engines were developed, tested, and installed; the ship itself was built; life-support, power systems, equipment, tools, seed stock...all were loaded aboard; the colonist volunteers had to be selected.

The ship was a symbol of hope, a last chance—one that had gutted Earth's economy at the worst possible time. After the slowship sailed away, filled with optimistic pioneers, a worldwide economic and environmental collapse led to a century of civil wars, famines, survivalist movements, and a succession of squabbling military dictators.

Eventually the solar flares died down, and Earth had begun to recover over the past few decades. Human civilization picked up the pieces, governments grew progressively stronger, finally reaching the current Golden Age under President Jurudu. (At least, that was what Jurudu's constant press releases claimed; Andre couldn't see that the people were noticeably more prosperous now than they had been under other regimes.)

With a common cause, every person had to chip in for future generations. "We sacrifice today to create a better tomorrow," was one of Jurudu's most common slogans. Andre would have preferred the President to focus his efforts more on agriculture, industry, education, and expansion of medical facilities, rather than on huge military and surveillance expenditures. But he kept his opinions to himself. He was pleased to be part of this project, working closely with one of the best theoretical physicists in the entire space program.

Embarrassed to have been caught daydreaming, Andre blanked the recording from the *Beacon*. "Sorry for the distraction, sir. I'll get back to work. These calculations show some promise. If they check out, I'll forward them to you. Might be useful for further development."

"Oh, no worries, young man." The physicist was smiling far too much. "And I won't be needing your equations." Dr. Max hooked his thumbs in his waistband, rocked back and forth on his heels, building the suspense. "After today, everything changes, Dr. Pellar. I've had a breakthrough—checked it and double-checked it. I'll give you my white paper as a courtesy—familiarize yourself with it. I already have a meeting set up with President Jurudu and the generals. You and I are going to be highly rewarded, provided you can help develop this concept and carry it through the testing and implementation stages."

Andre wished the scientist would get to the point. "I would be happy to help in any way possible, sir."

Dr. Max leaned closer as if sharing a secret, though only the two of them were in the laboratory. "I've worked out the new *faster-than-light drive*, Dr. Pellar. We'll be able to build spacecraft engines that are orders of magnitude faster than anything that's been developed before. Once we test the FTL and send out some sample probes, we can dispatch a ship of our own—our own colony ship! We'll reach Tau Ceti in no time, well ahead of the *Beacon*."

3

JORIE HAD SEEN THE *BEACON*'S Wall of Lives many times—she couldn't think of any place on the giant generation ship that she had not thoroughly explored in her fourteen years—but this was different.

The Captain brought her to the Wall in order to make a point.

Andropolis said, "You have to comprehend how the ship works, and know everything about us, if you want to be the next Captain."

Jorie gave the older woman a mischievous grin. "When did I ever say I wanted to be Captain?"

"You do, and don't pretend otherwise—or have I made the wrong choice as my protégée?"

"Don't worry, Captain—I'm planning to learn everything."

Andropolis gave a satisfied nod. "Do it, because as soon as we can gather more data on our new planet, there'll be a lot more for everyone to learn."

Jorie faced the transparent bulkhead wall in the Aquarium Room, raising her gaze to follow the columns of scribed names. The Wall of Lives curved up to the distant ceiling, a visible window into the toroidal water tanks that encircled the Habitation Decks. The water served not only as the supply reservoir for the colonists, but also provided shielding from cosmic radiation.

Such a vast amount of water would have drained a large lake on Earth, but lifting so much water out of a planetary gravity well would have been far too expensive. During the *Beacon*'s construction in orbit around the Moon, all the necessary water had been obtained by retrieving, dismantling, and thawing two small comets.

Segregated compartments of the toroidal water tanks preserved entire Earth ecosystems complete with algae, plankton, weeds, and a variety of edible fish: trout and salmon in this tank; anchovies, snapper, cod, halibut, and other fish in separate tanks at appropriate temperatures and salinities. The sleek forms flitted back and forth, exotic reminders of a lush and far-away world that Jorie had never known.

She had always wanted to see a live dolphin. The Noah's genetic library contained dolphin embryos, and she hoped they could be brought back, depending on the ocean conditions on Sarbras. Nobody knew whether the new seas could support Terran life...or if the planet had oceans at all. Even in the best case, they would have to establish the entire food chain, lay the foundations, start with the basic underpinnings.

Captain Andropolis said, "I need to emphasize just what a responsibility you will be shouldering, how much of an investment in hope, time, and lives has been put into this effort. Two centuries and about eight generations for us, thousands and thousands of lives aboard the *Beacon*, not to mention all those we left behind on Earth."

The old woman touched the etched letters, running her fingers along the column of names as high as she could reach, but they extended much farther up the towering glass aquarium wall. "These aren't just random names—they are a testament to everything that has been sacrificed so we could plant one seed on a new world."

The scribed words were so dense that the names blocked rectangular swatches of the wall. One framed section listed the 3,716 original colonists. "These are the ones from Earth, who boarded the *Beacon* and headed off on a one-way trip to a place no one had ever seen, knowing that not even their children's children would see the end of the voyage. Yet, still they left." The Captain looked at Jorie. "You and I were born into this—we had no choice. But those first people *volunteered*, knowing the gamble."

"We've lasted this long, and we're almost there," Jorie said. "I'm optimistic."

"A Captain has to be an optimist—don't ever lose that. But you'll need to be realistic and pragmatic as well. We know very little about Sarbras. What if we arrive only to find that we can't live there? Then what?"

Jorie had heard frightening questions like that over the years. Some people had made theoretical projections, while others continued to use the *Beacon*'s astronomical observation equipment to glean any possible details as they flew closer.

She pushed the fears aside. "Then we'll have to make do, Captain. The *Beacon* isn't going to turn around and head back home."

Andropolis nodded. "People have made grim projections for years, and we've tried to plan—but unlike all those others, you and your generation are actually going to face that reality. *You* will have to make the decisions and do whatever is necessary to keep the crew alive."

"You'll be with me there, Captain. It's only twenty-one years."

"Maybe, maybe not. Nothing is certain. That is why we plan."

Jorie looked up at the tens of thousands of names that had been inscribed over the past 196 years. Except for the first group from Earth, every single person memorialized on the Wall had been born aboard the *Beacon*, had grown up and died here, holding onto the long-term dream.

"When we arrive at Sarbras and build our cities," Andropolis mused, "we'll turn this wall into a monument to every single person who invested in our future. Captain Blake first proposed it, and every Captain since has committed to the idea. I suggest that you do it as well."

Jorie loved the idea. "That sounds beautiful. You and I will erect the monument together when we get to Sarbras."

4

WHEN DR. MAX CHAMBERS-OSAWA ASKED him to attend the high-level meeting at the President's palace, Andre felt intimidated. "But, sir, this is your presentation, your discovery. You're the head of the project, and besides…President Jurudu likes you already."

Dr. Max chuckled. "The President needs to like you as well, Andre. All the more reason for you to accompany me. This is a long-term project, and I intend to burden you with most of the management chores. I'll be *working*, and I can't always be bothered by nonsense meetings. I want the President and his generals to recognize you as my representative."

"I see your point, sir." Andre did not doubt that he was a valuable asset to the project. He had combed over Dr. Max's original calculations, rerunning the models to verify the physicist's conclusions. In doing so, Andre had discovered a slight but beneficial error that increased the predicted speed and efficiency of the FTL engines by 0.2 percent. Though the mistake annoyed and embarrassed Dr. Max, he was pleased with the performance improvement.

On the day of the meeting, Andre wore a new suit that cost more than he could afford, selected by his girlfriend,

Renee Sinha. Though the garment fit him well, he did not find it comfortable; he had never been the sort to wear suits, nor did he move in circles that required them, until now. For his own part, Dr. Max did not dress up for the high-level representatives, explaining that the import of his discovery would be readily apparent, and therefore should be more than enough to impress anybody.

The President's palace was a blocky yet ostentatious structure with marble columns and alabaster statues, towering paintings of President Jurudu as well as idyllic landscapes that showed how Earth had been and how it would be again. From these halls, Jurudu imposed his strict austerity measures worldwide, announced rigorous work requirements and productivity expectations in a series of plans that outlined the path to progress and prosperity. "We sacrifice today to create a better tomorrow." Unfortunately, their sacrifice had gone on for years, and the tomorrows did not seem much better.

As soon as the two arrived, Jurudu's staff ushered them into the President's private admin chambers. Dr. Max had already provided a cryptic description of his discovery when he set up the meeting, and the President was eager to hear what his pet project had produced.

As they entered the plush office, Andre on the heels of the physicist, Dr. Max bounced ahead, as if he were going to see a childhood friend rather than the most powerful man on Earth.

A trio of uniformed and heavily decorated men occupied chairs near the great desk: the generals in charge of the Surveillance & Security Bureau, Military Operations, and Police Operations, planetwide. Andre didn't understand the distinctions among the categories, but each officer wielded a great deal of power.

Even in the presence of the triumvirate of generals, President Jurudu dominated the room, drawing Andre's gaze like a magnet. He was a powerful, dark-skinned man with hair trimmed close to his head, thin eyebrows, and an equally thin moustache. His impeccable dark suit could barely contain his wide shoulders, and his hands looked powerful enough to squeeze blood from a stone. (Andre didn't doubt that he had tried.)

Jurudu rose from his desk and extended a hand as the physicist trotted toward him. "Dr. Chambers-Osawa, I was delighted to receive your report. It's a relief to hear from a project head who does not make excuses." His chuckle sounded like rocks rolling down a tiled hall.

"No excuses, Mr. President. I have done what you asked me to." Dr. Max turned, remembering his manners. "This is my assistant, Dr. Andre Pellar, to help with our presentation, and he will be instrumental in moving our project to its next phase."

"If there is a next phase," said the Surveillance & Security General.

Dr. Max glanced to the left, dismissed the man as if he were no more than a waiter. "There will be."

Andre dutifully opened the folders, handed presentation materials to the four men, and set up the display screen. He knew not to speak unless someone asked him a specific question.

Tossing his long, graying hair over his shoulder, Dr. Max began his talk, focused entirely on Jurudu. "Almost two hundred years ago, the slowship *Beacon* departed from Earth on an extended journey to another star system. That expensive vessel carried our best people and huge amounts of resources. In the years leading up to the launch, Earth sacrificed terribly to build that boondoggle ship." He sniffed. "I have never been convinced the cost was justified."

The three generals grumbled, and President Jurudu nodded. "What did we get for that effort? We should have devoted those resources to saving the rest of Earth's population, not just a handful."

Dr. Max sounded glib. "Water under the bridge, sir. That was centuries ago, and they didn't know any better. They were like old pioneers in rickety wagons crossing the country in search of the promised land. This, however, changes everything."

Grinning, he tapped the screen and displayed equations that meant nothing to the President and the generals. He continued, "But while those old pioneers continue to creak across the continent in covered wagons, imagine that we now have a hypersonic jet! With the faster-than-light engines I have designed, we can build a new ship and fill it with our own colonists. I predict we'll be able to launch within fifteen years, and still arrive at Tau Ceti before the *Beacon* does!"

"*If* it works," said the Military Operations General.

"It will."

"Prove it," President Jurudu said.

"That's precisely why I'm here. I'd like to develop a test probe, send it to Tau Ceti, and gather detailed images of the planet Sarbras. A proof-of-concept. Then, when *our* fast ship gets there full of *our* colonists, we'll be far better prepared than any of the people aboard that quaint generation ship."

With a nod from Dr. Max, Andre switched the image to an illustration that showed a rough blueprint of a new spacecraft, then moved on to a less-accurate but glorious rendition of the ship, followed by a chart of the local stars, and finally—because he knew it would be necessary—time and monetary projections.

The President's brow furrowed. "If we colonize that planet, can we take its resources and ship them back to Earth? Can we harvest food from the Tau Ceti planet and deliver it here to help our people?"

"Oh, no, Mr. President! The distance is too great, and the cost of travel would negate any savings."

"Then why should we waste money on this?" asked the Police Operations General. "The last Tau Ceti debacle destroyed our economy."

Dr. Max looked at the man as if he were a fool. "Because if there is going to be a second planet where humans make a new home, then it should be controlled *by us*, not by the group of people who drained away this world's resources in the first place."

Andre continued to flip the images, trying to keep up with the physicist's enthusiasm.

"Ah, manifest destiny," Jurudu said, pondering. "And I can be the first leader to place human footprints on an alien world, claim a whole star system for humanity."

"To what purpose, Mr. President?" the Military Operations general said. "It is so far away we could never effectively govern or even communicate with a second human planet."

"Your thinking is much too small, General. Only one person in all of human history can ever be *first*." The President locked eyes with Dr. Max and read everything he needed to know from his expression. "Build your probe and send it to Tau Ceti. Show me what your faster-than-light engines can do—and then we'll decide on the next step."

5

NIGEL ROSENBURG DESIGNED CITIES in his dreams, populating a planet he had never seen, developing buildings to fit within a landscape he could only imagine.

Rosenburg's showroom on Deck 17 was more like an art gallery than a working research lab. He invited Captain Andropolis and her protégée so he could show off an intricate new model he had spent months developing.

Rather than just conjecturing possible urban layouts and sketching rough blueprints for discussion and planning, Rosenburg went the full distance. His designs were more than flights of fancy: They showed what the *Beacon* colonists could achieve on Sarbras, and it gave them a chance to dream.

Even with a centuries-long journey ahead of them, the first few generations of crewmember-colonists had developed preliminary plans, but such schemes had always been too distant and theoretical to matter much.

Now that they were only about twenty years out, however, Nigel Rosenburg focused on concrete plans, mapping city grids with spacious, livable dwelling complexes and integrating them with transportation systems that could meet the needs of agriculture, mining, and industry. Before his death, old Captain Pellar had granted Rosenburg permission to spend his time creating one metropolis after another, based on numerous possible environments on Sarbras.

The city planner was a balding man with long mercurial eyebrows that rose like feathers above his eyes. Always cheerful, he would talk at great length about how much space was required for true happiness. He realized that some people would want to live close together in an urban environment (as they all currently did aboard the generation ship), while others would prefer open spaces, fields or forests.

Rosenburg's initial designs had been exotic and fanciful, but he was just getting warmed up. Since no one yet had any clear picture of the alien planet's geography, mineral resources, or climate, the canvas was blank and open. He let his ideas run wherever they wanted to go.

First, he designed a dramatic city of fairy-tale buildings that grew out of the walls of a gorge adorned with waterfalls. Hydroelectric generators tapped the plunging streams to power the city. Since preliminary data suggested that Sarbras had slightly lower gravity than Earth, Rosenburg stretched the design strengths of common construction materials to build gossamer skyscrapers, soaring minarets, and observation towers. Showing off his talents as an artist, Rosenburg painted pictures of his waterfall-canyon city surrounded by a veil of mist. He also built delicate, richly detailed models that filled a large showcase in his lab.

For his second design, conjecturing that Sarbras might be a cold world with large ice sheets, he proposed that the *Beacon* colonists could tunnel into the glaciers and excavate frozen grottoes for living areas. He modeled how the pioneers could process the ice to create air, water, and simple fuels; depending on the solar bombardment of the outer layers of the ice sheet, there could also be deuterium or tritium for power reactors. Even in subzero environments, he was certain that the hardy colonists could establish a thriving settlement, adding food algae to the walls, building hydroponics gardens with piped-in solar power; even, depending on the stability of the ice sheet, large grottoes where small livestock could roam.

Or, another case: if Sarbras were an ocean world, Rosenburg developed techniques to construct buildings on the ocean floor, sealed living modules that gradually blossomed into a full-blown metropolis under a necklace of protective domes, with open-air rafts tethered above.

The ideas inspired the dreams of everyone aboard. Jorie was convinced that if the colonists could live for more than two centuries on an enclosed starship, they could make a home just about anywhere.

Rosenburg led Captain Andropolis and Jorie into his work area, where his new model covered half of the table. Although they still had two decades to prepare, the city planner spent more time getting pragmatic for his new designs.

"This is a traditional settlement that we can easily build with the materials, tools, and expertise we have on board. I used simple, classic Earth cities as a model. For topography, let's assume a flat, arable landscape, perhaps grasslands. We'll build our city near a waterway." He raised his extravagant eyebrows so that the hairs looked like ferns unfurling, turned a paternal smile on Jorie. "I can list all the reasons for you, if you'd like?"

Jorie said, "No need—the reasons are straightforward, right out of the basic Earth history of urban development."

Rosenburg was taken aback by her answer, but obviously pleased. "Good, then." He paced around the table. "This is a best-case model, so assume that the soil is compatible for agriculture and that farmland will cover many acres outside of the city. We'll install a transportation system for farmers to deliver their crops to the larger cities. If there's a forest nearby—assuming that Sarbras even *has* trees—we can use the lumber for construction material."

"So many assumptions," Captain Andropolis said.

Rosenburg shrugged. "What else can we do?" He turned back to his model. "We'll build large power plants, industrial centers for processing materials, and mines wherever there are mineral resources." He stalled for a moment, then said, "I can't plan that in detail until we know the distribution of ores on the planet. Sorry about that, Captain."

"We'll be able to tweak this as we go along, Mr. Rosenburg," Andropolis said. "We still have twenty years."

He kept chattering. "The city center will be compact, and we'll expand vertically if the materials and the climate are amenable. The thousands of people aboard the *Beacon* have learned a great deal by living together so closely and efficiently for two hundred years."

Captain Andropolis smiled. "Given a whole planet of elbow room, we'll do just fine."

"And here, lest we forget." Rosenburg indicated the town square and a large monument that gleamed under the showroom light: a crystalline slab cut into an innovative geometric shape, tilted skyward. "This is the Wall of Lives. I've included that in every one of my designs."

Jorie leaned forward over the beautiful city model, imagining how this all could be real within her lifetime. Seeing her interest, Rosenburg said in a firm voice, "And you, young lady, will have to build my city."

✦

Although the *Beacon* sent an update message each year, transmissions from Earth arrived only intermittently. After so much time, Jorie figured that the people back there had mostly forgotten about them.

Over the centuries, the reports had been dire: solar flares, climatic destruction. The succession of upheavals made it appear that the entire ecosystem was doomed, that the human race—or at least civilization—would crumble.

Throughout the crisis, according to the sporadic reports, new leaders had appeared on Earth, usually warlords who enjoyed only brief reigns before being overthrown by someone with better promises or more powerful weapons. With the constant struggles to rebuild governments and societies, Jorie supposed that sending polite update messages to a long-gone ship was not high on anyone's priority list.

Whenever the *Beacon* did receive a new message, it came as a welcome relief and a matter of great interest.

Jorie was studying in the Captain's bridge office when the transmission arrived, and she and Andropolis eagerly sat before the screen. The speaker was a deep-voiced black man with firm, chiseled features and a striking air of confidence. "I am Earth's new President, Elé Jurudu. I am pleased to inform you that we have finally overcome our greatest obstacles. Earth is now unified under a single government and a single strong leader."

President Jurudu spoke from a well-appointed office, but his message included no external video of Earth's burgeoning cities, thriving factories, or restored parks. The *Beacon* listeners were supposed to take his statements on faith.

The man smiled, as if delivering good news. "Two years ago, I led a coup and defeated the forces that were holding us back. I have instituted austerity measures to help us climb out of our deep hole and rebuild civilization. Earth is about to begin a new Renaissance. We will recover, and we will grow strong again."

"That message is ten years old," Jorie pointed out. "I wonder what's happened since."

Jurudu continued in a harder voice. "Using the best technology available, the *Beacon* embarked on a long one-way voyage and took with it our prime resources, our finest creative and scientific minds. After you left us, Earth suffered greatly from devoting its wealth and resources to building your vessel, but now we are recovering. Our nightmare is over, and Earth is ready for a new dawn." He folded his hands, smiled, and ended the transmission.

Jorie considered the man's choice of words, his tone. "It sounds like they're blaming us for their problems."

"We're far away, and we can't defend ourselves or refute his claims," Andropolis said. "But I disagree with his assessment of us. The *Beacon* was a landmark of human cooperation and shared sacrifice. We saw a need, faced the challenge, and accomplished something wonderful for our race as a whole. Apparently, that spirit of cooperation didn't last. I'm glad we got out when we did."

The Captain let out a sigh. "I'll broadcast it shipwide and let everyone draw their own conclusions. We've seen Jurudu's type before. He may be no better than any of the other leaders."

"That makes me sad, but it doesn't really matter to us," Jorie said. "We'll never go back there, and we have a clean slate—a world that we can't mess up."

6

AFTER HIS INTENSE WORKDAYS on the FTL project, Andre enjoyed evenings in his austere apartment with Renee Sinha, an intelligent, opinionated, and passionate woman who had chosen to become his partner. He didn't know what she saw in him, but after so many years of deprivation, people no longer dreamed of fairy-tale romances, choosing instead to find a match that guaranteed food, shelter, and stability.

Renee put in a full shift in a chemical-processing factory and also worked part-time as a hired driver. With Andre's responsibilities in Complex Alpha, especially now that President Jurudu had given a green light to developing a proof-of-concept FTL probe, their schedules did not often match, which made him appreciate the evenings when they could be together.

He and Renee shared a meal of bland food: noodles with spices, watery broth, and a few bits of meat sprinkled with concentrated protein nuggets. Andre was a dutiful research deputy, and he knew to hold his opinions in check, voicing no criticisms, even in private. He never talked about his work.

Renee, on the other hand, had too many opinions to keep to herself, and she often spoke at great length and with great conviction, as if she believed Andre was in a position to change the world. Now that he was working on a project of vital importance, and actually met with President Jurudu, she thought he had genuine influence.

"Why do we view the *Beacon* as competition?" she asked. "All of Earth joined in that project. Everyone agreed it was a good idea. Our hopes and prayers went with them. And I'm glad—*glad* that they're almost there."

"But if our project works," Andre said, "those pioneers don't have to be so alone. We could join them and build a colony together on Sarbras."

Lifting a forkful of noodles from the plate, she leaned over with a skeptical frown. "Sharing resources and building a colony together? You think that's what President Jurudu has in mind?"

He glanced away. "No, I suppose not."

"Consider what the *Beacon* colonists proved, just by staying alive for all that time! They've beaten the odds. They learned how to survive for two centuries in an enclosed man-made ecosystem. Imagine the bravery! No one on Earth dreams that big anymore. All we do is try to survive year after year and endure the next set of austerity measures."

Andre realized that he didn't disagree. He spent a great deal of time wondering what might have happened if his ancestors had joined the colony ship along with those other Pellars. However, because he worked directly for President Jurudu, he felt obligated to say, "We're surviving—isn't that good enough? A hundred years ago, that wasn't a sure thing. It's why we built the *Beacon* and sent it away, because we feared the human race would die out. Extinct." He ate another mouthful. "We aren't living in a paradise, Renee, but we're alive, and things are sure to get better."

With a bitter laugh, she pushed aside her bowl of noodles. "Oh, Andre, I know you have to say that, but you don't have to accept everything they tell you. 'We sacrifice today to create a better tomorrow'? Do you really believe that? I was attracted to you because of your intelligence. Don't be passive and accept the status quo."

Andre wasn't very hungry, yet because of the austerity measures he did not dare let a scrap of food go to waste. He dutifully ate his meal.

To encourage him, Renee queued up the *Beacon*'s recent message. "Isn't it remarkable that even after all this time, they keep sending us messages of hope?" They watched the cheerful announcement of Captain Pellar being appointed to the leadership role. "You're related to that man—don't you feel a connection to him? Thousands of those original colonists still have relatives here on Earth. Most may have forgotten how courageous their ancestors were—but not all of us. We pray for those explorers, and we're with them in spirit. The *Beacon* colonists are going to achieve their dreams after all!"

Thinking her naïve, he said, "Exactly. How could those left behind not resent that?"

7

OVER THE SLOWSHIP'S VOYAGE, there had been good Captains and mediocre ones. Jorie vowed that she would be the *best*—especially if she was supposed to lead during the first years of the new colony.

Each crewmember-colonist received intensive education and practice in order to preserve the collective levels of expertise, to hone their skills, and maintain the colony readiness for when they reached their new world. Teacher after teacher hammered in the fundamental principle: "We must not forget what we know."

At the very beginning of the voyage, Captain Rochelle had been keenly aware that subsequent generations could lose vital skills and experience. When they arrived at Sarbras many generations later, they would need experts in mining, metallurgy, industry, electromagnetics, meteorology. For centuries, however, none of the students had any chance to put their planetary knowledge into practice. Nevertheless, they learned for themselves and taught their children, who would pass on the teachings to their children….

Jorie wanted to be more widely knowledgeable than anyone else, have a solid background on all the ship's major systems, understand the big picture. She already had a full slate of classes in science and industry, and she spent hours each day with Captain Andropolis learning about leadership.

Whenever the Captain had specific meetings for her, Jorie was excused from her formal classes, although not from the homework. Andropolis insisted that she review the day's lessons and learn the material as well as, if not better than, her fellow students. Jorie never complained, but threw herself into the effort with all of her heart.

Now, she accompanied the Captain to the greenhouse dome to hear the Noah's monthly review. The well-lit dome was the *Beacon*'s largest park, filled with the smell of vegetation, humid air, mulch and fertilizer. Trickling irrigation streams ran along the ground, making the place a delight. Under the overarching dome, the plants grew in a layer of soil that was carefully fertilized and maintained—dirt that came from Earth itself.

In addition to maintaining the ship's inventory of seeds and embryos, the Noah also enhanced food strains and developed ways to increase edible biomass from the greenhouses. Thanks to the efforts of his predecessors, the greenhouse crops were just as efficient as the water-grown hydroponics trays, which also produced fruits and vegetables.

When they arrived, the Noah paid special attention to Jorie. "I decided to generate the seeds from five birch trees, and my assistant and I planted them here in the big dome. It should be tall enough for them to thrive." He heaved a long, wistful sigh. "It'll be nice to have birches."

"I've seen stands of birches in images." Jorie recalled forest landscapes of spindly, white-barked trees with golden leaves.

She had read poetic descriptions of the sweet smell of fallen birch leaves, how the bark could be peeled off like paper....

"Go have a look," the Noah said. "Carrick can tell you all about the trees." Jorie wondered how much there was to know about birch trees, but she sensed the Noah wanted a word alone with the Captain, so she trudged across the soft grass.

At a stand of small trees as high as her waist, she spotted Carrick Platt, a young man her age, at the edge of an irrigation canal, digging a long furrow in the soil. He was covered with a thick slurry of mud—smears across his shirt, his arms, knees, and feet.

Seeing him, she laughed. "You're filthy!"

Carrick showed no embarrassment. "It's dirt. Dirt is where life comes from. And this is real dirt...earth from Earth. You should respect it." Teasingly, he threw a clod at her, which spattered across her blouse. When she cried out, Carrick said, "You must be the one the Noah wanted me to meet."

Indignant about the mud and the comment, Jorie wiped the dirt from her shoulder. "He said you were going to tell me about birch trees."

"He said that, did he?" Carrick asked. "They're trees. I could give you the scientific name, describe where they used to grow on Earth, explain the germination process...but it's probably not all that interesting."

"Probably not." She knelt down near the stream bank to see what he was doing. As soon as Carrick turned his head away, she scooped up a handful of mud and dumped it over the back of his head.

And that was just the start.

✦

On the observatory deck, the astronomers were intent on their instruments while Captain Andropolis and Jorie remained in the back of the room, careful not to interfere. The Captain insisted, "It is important to be present for significant events."

The chief astronomer explained with exaggerated patience, "The planet is transiting Tau Ceti. It'll happen more often now as our approach aligns with the ecliptic." He seemed unaware of who Jorie was, or why a teenaged girl would be there. "We've enhanced the *Beacon*'s telescopes over the years so that we can see more of our new planet. There's a lot of dust around the outskirts of the Tau Ceti system, obscuring the view for now. Our resolution will improve as we come into the system."

"And what does the transit show us?" the Captain asked, probably for Jorie's benefit, but Jorie had already taken two years of astronomical training.

"We can get a spectrum of the atmosphere. We'll have only a fraction of a second to gather data, but that will yield significant information. We have the baseline Tau Ceti spectrum, and when the planet crosses the star's limb, we can separate the two spectra, which will tell us more about Sarbras."

Sarbras…even its name, a perfect palindrome, spelled the same forward and backward, implying "there and back again" for the planet. Except the *Beacon* colonists would not be going back to Earth. Ever. They had to accept whatever was there.

The primary telescope screen combined numerous images gathered from the large reflectors, as well as tethered outrigger satellites that increased the observational baseline. Jorie could see the grainy, speckled image of Tau Ceti—yellow-orange, slightly smaller than Earth's sun—and the small dot as Sarbras crossed the face of the star. The astronomical team compared the spikes and bands on the spectrographic traces and subtracted out the baseline of the star's spectrum, to yield only the lines absorbed by the planet's atmosphere.

"Looks like Sarbras has all the right elements, as we expected: nitrogen, oxygen, water vapor, CO_2, trace gases." The astronomer looked closer. "A little higher sulfur content than we expected, possibly implying volcanic activity." He glanced up. "We'll need some time to study this, Captain."

"Keep looking," Andropolis said. "By the time we arrive, we'll know all we possibly can about the planet."

PART TWO

8

200 years since the Beacon's *departure from Earth.*
17 years to scheduled arrival at Tau Ceti.

THE PROOF-OF-CONCEPT FTL PROBE didn't look like much, from an aesthetics standpoint: a set of Dr. Max's new-design engines (collectively the size of a three-story building) topped with a small sensor package, and not much else. But the beauty was inside, a symphony of artful and sophisticated physics.

Over the years since President Jurudu approved the project, Andre had worked closely with Dr. Max, shouldering the administrative duties at Complex Alpha and monitoring the development of the engines through a dozen different test stages. While Dr. Max had created the original breakthrough, he waved his hands through the big picture of the FTL project; the physicist had no patience for the complicated and often frustrating management chores. Now that his hard "brain work" was done, he spent a lot of time at black-tie state functions with the President and his staff.

Andre was left to supervise work teams, oversee procurement operations, and prioritize funds and manpower. He had never liked to draw attention to himself, and rubbing shoulders with high-level diplomats made him uncomfortable. He just wanted to live a quiet life and manage as best he could.

Though her job was not nearly as flashy as his, Renee remained energetic and passionate about many things. When they did find time to be together, she told him about people she'd driven around, or she discussed routine activities at the chemical plant, but she was most interested in the new friends she'd met outside of work. Renee kept wanting him to join her and her companions at a coffee club in the evenings or for a soup lunch in a government cafeteria, but he was too busy preparing the test probe, especially now that the launch date had been set.

Even with President Jurudu's full support, building the FTL probe took four years. Though the work was technically on schedule, Dr. Max often paced back and forth in his lab, frustrated that plans on paper took so long to implement in actuality. Once, in response to his grumbling, President Jurudu had told the physicist with a paternal smile, "I understand completely, my friend. My prosperity plans seem so easily achievable when I write them up, but you can't count on other people to work as hard as you do. That's why we have to watch everyone so closely."

The primary bottleneck was that Earth's space program—at its pinnacle during the construction and launch of the *Beacon*—had lain fallow for two centuries, all that knowledge and expertise lost, the industrial facilities shelved or retooled; nowadays, it was nearly impossible to find anyone with practical aerospace experience. Why would anyone bother? Space science was no longer a viable field of study with Earth's at-home difficulties so much more prominent.

Thus, the FTL project had started from scratch, but the President's command opened all the necessary doors. There was some initial public criticism about Jurudu squandering funds and resources that should have been devoted to improving the standard of living, but they were quickly silenced.

Renee also insisted that the FTL project was unnecessary, but for her own reasons. Often, she and Andre would sit in their apartment and debate into the late hours, even though he had to get up early and get to Complex Alpha. "The *Beacon* is already on its way," she said. "Why would you trample on their dreams like that?"

"I'm sending a *probe*, Renee. We just want to get a look at the Tau Ceti planet."

She sniffed. "No, you don't. It won't stop there, and you know it."

In fact, he was sure it would not, but he didn't admit that to Renee. He tried a different argument. "For the good of the human spirit, shouldn't we try a grand project again? Shouldn't we let ourselves dream after this long nightmare of hardship?"

Renee had leaned over and kissed him. "That's a beautiful sentiment, Andre, and I agree wholeheartedly—but are you talking about *humanity's* dreams, or Jurudu's dreams?"

He frowned. "Can't they be the same?"

She gave a sigh like a parent dealing with a particularly thick child. "I love you Andre, but you really must pull your head out of your orifice."

✦

Though he still felt out of his depth, Andre joined Dr. Max for the ceremony at the President's palace, where the important people could watch the probe's departure from orbit.

Andre had asked if Renee could be his special guest at the reception, although she did not seem keen on attending. However, when the President's staff sent stacks of paperwork to be filled out—approval forms, authorizations for intensive background checks and security clearances—she declined, saying it simply wasn't worth all that effort just to have a glass of champagne and watch a spacecraft move across a screen

Feeling alone during the reception, Andre talked with a few well-dressed people, answered politely when he was spoken to, and drifted around the lavish room to avoid notice. He kept to the edge of the hall, drank a little too much, and wished he was back home.

When the time came, everyone fell silent to listen to filtered announcements from the six spacesuited crewmembers, a newly trained group of orbital workers who, four years earlier, would never have dreamed of going into space. The construction captain transmitted the probe's readiness, and screens showed the countdown. President Jurudu wished them luck.

The space workers disengaged the probe from its orbiting construction gantry and nudged the ungainly craft away from the structure with bursts of maneuvering jets. When it drifted free, the probe aligned itself, using navigation locks to fix the course on Tau Ceti, which was an unremarkable star in a sea of stars.

Andre moved to stand beside Dr. Max, holding his breath. Together, the two men watched as the initial rockets ignited beneath the unmanned probe. The first stages were just standard engines to accelerate the spacecraft out of Earth orbit. Astronauts on the station platform tracked the probe as it moved away at increasing speed.

Dr. Max was grinning.

With a searing blue-white flash, the faster-than-light engines came online, and the probe flickered away in an instant, like a dragonfly lost in the bright sunlight. The observers applauded as soon as President Jurudu applauded.

He made his well-rehearsed speech. "It is said that when Alexander the Great had defeated the known world, he wept for there were no more worlds to conquer. I have taken Earth in my embrace and saved it from self-destruction, but we must reach farther and dream harder. An entire new star system is ours for the taking, for the good of humanity. We must leave *our* mark there and build a new empire under *our* flag.

"The people aboard the *Beacon* departed two hundred years ago and still haven't reached their destination. Now, we can get there in a few months." He let out a condescending chuckle. "If this probe is successful, we will build a gigantic colony ship of our own and head for Tau Ceti. We can get there first and achieve in a month what our rivals took centuries to accomplish."

He shook his head, and his voice held anger. "The *Beacon* project caused tremendous hardship to those of us who remained behind. If those cowards had helped their fellow man instead of fleeing a sinking ship, if they had devoted those resources to *humanity's* needs instead of their selfish goals, we could all have gone to Tau Ceti much more swiftly and without so much suffering."

Grumbles rippled around the room. Then, with a wide grin, President Jurudu raised his champagne glass and turned to the physicist. "A toast to Dr. Max Chambers-Osawa and his great breakthrough." He took a gulp of champagne, then hurled the glass at the starry screen, where the probe had already vanished. The crowd roared and did likewise. As did Andre.

✦

Since the automated probe flew faster than the speed of light, it outraced any radio transmissions to or from the distant star. The project team had to wait for the probe to make the round-trip journey before they could see any results at all: five weeks out to Tau Ceti, where the suite of analytics would take images of the star system and the planet; then, if all systems functioned properly, five weeks to fly back to Earth and deliver the data. If the probe simply sent a signal with its observations from Tau Ceti itself, the transmission would take nearly twelve years to travel across the interstellar void.

Two and a half months was a trivial amount of time for such a momentous flight. Nevertheless, each day dragged on, and Andre felt as if he were holding his breath. So much rode on this one set of results.

Dr. Max was eager to confirm that his starship engines could drive a spacecraft 11.9 light years and back in a reasonable amount of time, while Andre wanted to see what the probe learned about the Tau Ceti planet. The *Beacon* had set course for that enigmatic world, knowing almost nothing about it—the greatest and most expensive gamble in human history. If Sarbras was not, in fact, habitable, then all that investment, all those hopes and lives would have been wasted.

While waiting for the projected return date, Andre agreed to go out for drinks with Renee and her friends. He found them an intense lot, full of impractical solutions for the world's problems; they didn't seem to know what to do with him, though, and Andre was too preoccupied to be very good company. Renee nudged him in the ribs, tried to get him to participate in the conversation, but he shook his head, apologizing, "I'm sorry. This waiting is just driving me mad."

She laughed in disbelief. "The colonists aboard the *Beacon* had to wait for *two centuries*. You can endure a few weeks."

He was interested to learn that several of Renee's friends also traced their lineage back to families aboard the generation ship, and they were proud to call themselves "stepchildren of the *Beacon*." Hearing this made him feel warm inside, and he told them with a hint of pride that the slowship's current Captain (according to the latest transmissions) was his distant relative. "And I'm proud to be part of the extended family," he said.

✦

The probe returned on schedule, much to Dr. Max's delight. He and Andre holed up at Complex Alpha, poring over the new data the sensors had collected. Mankind's first close-up view of an extrasolar planetary system!

The automated probe had undershot Tau Ceti, arriving well outside the dust-enshrouded star—an error that amounted to less than 1%, so Dr. Max was not overly concerned, although the probe's images of the new planet were of disappointingly low resolution.

Centuries-old observations had already indicated that Sarbras possessed a breathable atmosphere and oceans with liquid water—excellent news all around. When launching the FTL probe, Dr. Max's team had known too little about the planetary system to calculate the Sarbras orbit with any accuracy, and the new images showed only a murky blur: a sphere with clouds in its atmosphere and occasional glimpses of land masses—no panoramic landscapes of the alien world that was destined to become humanity's second home. Nevertheless, this data was far better than any they had previously possessed.

Dr. Max studied the planetary images, but he was more interested in deconstructing the FTL engines to discover any signs of strain or possible failures or inconsistencies. Sarbras held very little interest for him. As far as he was concerned, the probe's FTL engines had worked; therefore, scaled-up engines could take a much larger craft filled with their own colonists to Sarbras.

"The galaxy is now open to the human race!" the President announced.

9

FOR TWO CENTURIES, THE COLONISTS looked to their Captains for continuity, safety, and guidance. Each Captain from Rochelle through Andropolis had made sure the engines functioned properly; the life-support and recycling systems operated without incident; the greenhouses and aquariums provided sufficient food.

After four years of study, Jorie had impressed Captain Andropolis enough that on her eighteenth birthday she was officially appointed the Deputy Captain. The announcement surprised no one aboard the ship.

To celebrate the appointment, Andropolis invited Jorie to suit up and go outside the ship with her. Together, they would stand on top of their world and look across the cosmos.

Most people aboard had little occasion to go outside. Engineers and maintenance crews made monthly expeditions across the hull, but they were an isolated lot, preferring their own company in the lower decks. The *Beacon*'s average crewmember never had such an opportunity. Suiting up for discretionary trips was the Captain's prerogative.

In preparation, Andropolis put Jorie through five separate practice runs in the simulation chamber, tested and fitted one of the environment suits just for her, drilled her on the hazards of hard vacuum and cosmic radiation, and ran her through thirty different unlikely but dangerous accident scenarios.

Jorie paid close attention, determined to pass every test, but her mood was giddy. She couldn't wait to have a real adventure and tell Carrick about it; it would certainly be more exciting than the young man's experiences in the greenhouse dome, the Noah's plans for cross-breeding legumes, the test plots of new seeds they germinated for eventual planting on Sarbras.

Wearing their bulky suits, Jorie and the Captain entered the maintenance airlock, standing together in the cramped chamber. The last time she had seen this airlock in use was more than four years earlier, during Captain Pellar's funeral. This was a much more joyous occasion.

As the Captain sealed the interior hatch, Jorie saw the excitement reflected on the other woman's face from behind her faceplate. Kora Andropolis looked like a young girl, her eyes sparkling. Through the helmet radio, the older woman said, "Are you ready for a new experience, Deputy Captain?"

"Absolutely, Captain." Jorie's heart was pounding. Though she breathed slowly, she could hear each exhalation echo in the helmet. The air smelled dry, flat, and metallic, not at all like the humid environment inside the greenhouse domes, but Jorie didn't mind. She was going *outside!*

After the air drained back into the storage tanks, the outer airlock door slid open to the wide universe. Jorie let the Captain go first, and Andropolis moved forward, climbing out of the chamber and planting a magnetic boot on the expanse of hull plates. Jorie followed her, imitating her movements, and stepped out into…absolute openness.

Her entire life had been enclosed within walls. Even the large Aquarium Room, the cargo-storage bays, and the high greenhouse domes imposed boundaries on what she could see. Now, for the first time ever, Jorie saw a horizon: the slowship's hull was an endless plane of interlocked metal plates studded with modules and protrusions, sensor panels, whip-like probe antennae. The *Beacon* was an enormous ship, the size of a small asteroid, having been constructed in lunar orbit because it was much too large to be launched after it was built. Now, the curve of her whole world dropped off into infinity.

"Welcome to the universe, Jorie Taylor," the Captain said.

Just looking out into the unending ocean of bright stars made Jorie dizzy and disoriented. She could still feel the solid ship beneath her boots, but everything else in all directions fell away to forever. Other than the *Beacon*, she saw no anchor point, no way in which to orient herself. She swallowed hard. "I hope you have the course set straight, Captain. I can't see where we're going or where we've been. We really are in the middle of nowhere."

The Captain's voice held a deep sense of wonder. "On the contrary, Jorie, we're in the middle of *everywhere*." She got her bearings, looked at the star patterns, and told Jorie to scout the constellations herself. "You've studied these. See if you can find Cetus."

Jorie found the pattern, sketched the imaginary lines that connected the bright stars, outlining a shape that the ancient Greeks had seen as a huge whale in the night sky. As she looked now, she noted that one of the stars in the constellation pattern was brighter than what the library charts showed, the one named with the Greek letter tau.

"That's it—Tau Ceti." Jorie extended her arm and pointed with a gloved finger. "It still looks far away."

"Yes, that's where we're going. Back there behind us"— the Captain turned around, extending both of her hands to encompass a wide swath of the sky. "Can you find the constellation Boötes? From where we are now, Earth's sun is just a third-magnitude star in Boötes. It'll stand out as an anomaly from the pattern you memorized on the old charts."

Jorie scrutinized the sky, found the elongated spear-head shape that the Greeks called Boötes the hunter, but she couldn't spot Sol. "I'm surprised the constellations still look the same, even from this far away."

"Even ten light years is still just a tiny gap on the scale of the Galaxy," the Captain said. "Here, let me show you." She guided Jorie's gloved hand, tracing patterns among the stars until she finally identified the third-magnitude dot. "There's our old sun."

It didn't look special at all. Jorie said, "Do you think they'll ever send another expedition to Tau Ceti?"

"Maybe in the far, far future, once we've proved that it can be done. And we're going to prove it. Many of the people back on Earth would not have bet on us surviving even this long, but because we've been so careful, because we've scrimped and recycled and taken care of our limited resources, we still have plenty of food. Our life-support systems and power generators are operating above design specs, and even our remaining fuel supplies are far above estimates. Over the voyage, our scientists have improved the efficiency of our engines and scooped up additional hydrogen on our journey to be used as fuel."

Jorie brightened. "If we have the extra fuel, can't we accelerate? We could get to Sarbras faster."

"Yes, we could shave a few years off our journey, but then we'd burn our reserves. I agree with Captain Pellar before me. For our survival we should keep those reserves in case we need them. We've spent two centuries in transit—why get impatient now?"

"I guess you're right, Captain," Jorie said, "but still it's hard to wait and wait all my life…all your life."

"We're not just *waiting* to no purpose, Jorie. We are *living*. We're not simply a lost generation, not a stopgap on the way to a new colony—nor were any of the generations before us. We all *lived* aboard this ship. We are who we are, and our lives matter as they are. You have to understand that as Captain."

Jorie thought about that, felt it resonate in her heart, and turned to look toward Tau Ceti, focused her attention on the bright yellow star. "I won't forget, Captain."

10

SHORTLY AFTER THE SUCCESSFUL RETURN of the Tau Ceti probe, President Jurudu signed a decree that expanded the boundaries of Complex Alpha and transferred thousands more workers to the project.

Dr. Max spent his time designing the full-scale FTL colony ship that would carry a thousand loyalist pioneers to Tau Ceti, and he could not be bothered with management distractions. Without asking him ahead of time, Dr. Max appointed Andre as chief administrator. Though Andre did not want the assignment or believe he had the proper expertise, President Jurudu authorized the promotion and asked not to be bothered further with the details. A brushfire war in Southeast Asia kept the President's attention focused as he brought in armed forces to impose peace and stability.

And so, Andre became the new administrator of Complex Alpha, which quadrupled in size, transitioning from a theoretical think-tank to a gigantic outpost with a breathtaking goal.

Entire villages near the outskirts of the compound were evacuated, the inhabitants reassigned to space-program tasks. Large excavating machines came in to flatten the landscape and build new barracks, roads, rails, power plants. Jurudu allowed the diversion of construction teams and engineering crews from building two large hydroelectric dams, assigning them instead to construct launchpads for shuttles that would ferry materials up to the assembly site in orbit.

Andre was at a loss as to how to manage such an immense movement of personnel and materials, so he studied records of the only comparable project he knew: the *Beacon*'s construction.

Andre couldn't help but admire those old pioneers, even though Jurudu and Dr. Max continued to paint them as exploiters and opportunists. Yes, the generation ship had been the most enormous expense in human history, but while the

Beacon might have contributed to the strain on the worldwide economy, it was by no means the *only* factor that had brought about the collapse.

In those days, the human race had been unified by a common hope and goal. Now, however, the public attitude was different. When President Jurudu announced his vision, people would draw together as they were told, but Andre doubted they would put their hearts into it as the original project participants had....

✦

As soon as Dr. Max was ready to unveil detailed designs of the sleek new ship, President Jurudu made an official speech with great fanfare, although the project was already well underway. In a broad valley, he commanded the largest worldwide audience in his sixteen years of unchallenged rule. A sea of human faces greeted him with cheers and applause.

"Our world, beloved though it may be, is old and worn. Earth has sheltered us long enough, and we have taken all she has to give. It's time for the human race to leave the nest and claim a new home. Sarbras!"

Jurudu gestured to the expansive screen behind him. His specialists had taken the FTL probe's blurry data and modified the images to depict the Tau Ceti planet as a beautiful place with sparkling oceans, verdant continents, and billowy white clouds. Andre had studied the original low-res images himself and knew that these new versions were pure fancy— but perhaps the people needed fanciful optimism, if they were being asked to sacrifice even more. For a better tomorrow.

"A paradise full of resources, untamed lands for brave pioneers," the President continued. "And we must get there before the *Beacon* colonists arrive and take it all for their selfish ends."

Although Andre would not have characterized the original slowship project like that, he knew Dr. Max agreed with the sentiment. Puffed up by the success of his FTL probe test, the older physicist insisted that Tau Ceti was theirs for the

be there waiting for them when they arrive at Sarbras—if all goes as planned." And Andre knew that, under Jurudu's command, all *would* go as planned.

The physicist was not convinced. "Why in the world would we want to do that?" When Andre persisted, Dr. Max sent him away and left the decision to Jurudu.

Troubled, the President called Andre to his offices and said without preamble, "If we do as you suggest, we would sacrifice our element of surprise. I see no advantage in informing them of our plans."

Andre stood straight before the imposing wooden desk. "We already hold all the cards, Mr. President. On the timeline, the *Conquistador* will have four years to map the planet, claim the best areas for ourselves, build and secure a strong settlement. Then, when the *Beacon* arrives, we can incorporate them into our colony, make use of their equipment and resources. We want their cooperation. Wouldn't it be better to give them a chance to prepare for the idea?"

Seeing Jurudu's continuing skepticism, Andre took a different approach, one that had made an impression on Dr. Max. "Even if we send a message now, Mr. President, it'll still take nearly eleven years before our transmission reaches them. Earth has suffered for centuries since the *Beacon* left us—wouldn't you like them to know that we've beaten them? That after their incredibly long journey, we've already raced past them and succeeded?"

The President raised his eyebrows. "You suggest we gloat, Dr. Pellar?"

"I wouldn't put it quite so bluntly..."

Jurudu smiled. "Maybe it's good for them to be aware of the harm they've done to our world, and know that they can't do it again on Sarbras. We need to tell them they must be prepared to cooperate with us and abide by our ideals." He looked up, capturing Andre with his gaze. "We are still on schedule? To reach Tau Ceti first?"

"Yes, Mr. President."

Jurudu nodded slowly. "Very well, draft the message for me, and I will approve the words. I trust I can leave the transmission process to you?"

"Of course, Mr. President. You placed me in charge of Complex Alpha. I can handle sending a simple message."

✦

Wanting to be away from the fenced-in offices while he chose the appropriate wording, Andre went home. Although he knew Jurudu would revise the text, he had a good idea of what to say.

He could not downplay the significance of the construction and imminent launch of the *Conquistador*, nor what it might mean to the colonists aboard the generation ship. However, when he sent the President's announcement, he intended to append the complete data files from the FTL probe (without asking permission); that would give the *Beacon* colonists all available information about the mysterious new world. At least it would allow them to plan.

When he entered his apartment, he was delighted to find Renee there; he had missed seeing her the past several times, since she was out with her friends. He noticed immediately that her face was bruised, her left eye nearly swollen shut; she had tried, without success, to cover the discoloration with makeup.

He ran to her. "Renee, what happened?"

"It doesn't matter." She brushed him aside as he followed her around the room, deeply concerned. "I got in a fight. You know how my friends like to debate. It got out of hand."

"Why didn't you tell me? I could have been here!"

She frowned at him. "Andre, when have you been here?" His heart sank as she continued. "You devote every day to taking away the triumph from those people aboard the *Beacon*, from your own cousins! Don't they deserve it? They gave up everything and invested generations on their voyage."

He felt testy to hear that she resented him and his work. "And we stayed here on Earth for the same amount of time—it wasn't a picnic for us, either! And now we've developed a faster engine. Neither one was easy. We deserve what we create for ourselves."

Renee would not be swayed. "So, a farmer cuts down a forest, clears a field, plows the soil, plants his crops, weeds them, tends them…and just before he can bring in the harvest, bandits steal all the grain. Are you saying the bandits deserve the harvest as much as the farmer does?"

Andre was shocked. "Are you comparing us to bandits?"

She gave him a cool shrug. "Aren't you trying to steal a planet right out from under their noses after they've spent two hundred years getting there?" Even though he had just gotten back to the apartment, Renee gathered her jacket and went to the door. "I'm going out with my friends."

Recalling the protest that had erupted during the President's speech and the rough response of the security troops, he suspected how Renee had been beaten and bruised.

"But I hoped…I'd like to spend some time with you."

"You'd better spend some time alone thinking," she said and left.

11

WITH ITS ENCLOSED EARTH FORESTS, meadows, and plots of flowers, the *Beacon*'s central terrarium dome was highly coveted for weddings. Since Jorie Taylor was the Captain's official deputy and protégée, she had enough pull to request the spot when she married Carrick Platt.

Jorie's parents and brother Steven were there, along with Carrick's mother and his two young sisters. They gathered beside the running irrigation stream where Jorie had first met him. His birch trees now stood nearly three meters tall, reaching slowly up to the dome high above.

She focused her attention on her husband-to-be, the young man who'd splashed her with mud on the first day they'd met. *Earth from Earth.* He spent his days tending the trees, studying the seed library, and dreaming of the legendary forests on old Earth. Over the past four years, Carrick had given her an appreciation for the preciously guarded ecosystem, and her understanding now went far beyond the facts she had learned in her classes. Since she would eventually become the *Beacon*'s Captain, Jorie knew she had to be invested in the mission, not just with her mind, but with all her heart and soul. Carrick made certain she didn't forget that.

The two were eighteen, nearly nineteen—old enough to settle down and start their own family. As soon as they had decided to get married, Jorie and an awkward Carrick presented themselves before Captain Andropolis. When they made their announcement, the old woman did not look at all surprised. "You two may have agonized over the decision for months, but the rest of us saw it coming a light-year away." She chuckled. "I'm glad you're finally getting down to business."

"Does that mean we have your blessing, Captain?" Jorie asked.

Carrick was alarmed by the question. He whispered to Jorie, "Do we need it?"

"Of course you don't," Andropolis said, "but it never hurts to have the ship's Captain on your side. And I will perform the ceremony myself, along with the Noah."

Carrick's eyes went wide, and he swallowed hard, but Jorie couldn't keep from grinning. "That would be acceptable, Captain."

Now, in the high forest dome, the air exchangers operated at their highest capacity because of the gathered crowd. Even so, the moving air was not enough to generate a breeze.

Jorie looked up and saw a few of the leaves rustling and she tried to imagine wind whispering through a forest on Earth. Poets had described the chatter of aspen leaves, the soft sigh of a breeze through dense pines, but she had never heard it herself. Maybe Sarbras would have native forests, huge stands of alien trees. Or the colonists would plant their own trees from seeds preserved in the Noah's library bank. Someday....

When Jorie looked at Carrick, he seemed very young and boyish. This man was going to be her husband? *Yes,* she thought. *Yes, he is.*

Traditionally, families aboard the *Beacon* were limited to two children, in order to maintain the population level at its stable point of three thousand people, which did not stress their food supply or life-support systems. In order to ensure genetic diversity for when they reached Sarbras, each couple was encouraged to have one natural child and a second artificially inseminated from the large sperm bank that the *Beacon* had brought along upon departure from Earth.

Now, Captain Andropolis spoke the words of the wedding ceremony, a familiar blessing that had been used for colonist couples, generation after generation. "Our lives are braided together to become stronger. Each family is a thread in the fabric of our safety net. You two join in a stronger knot that can never be untied—and you will create strands of your own."

The Noah picked up the ceremony. The silver-haired man still looked bright and vibrant, as if he drew personal energy from all of his trees and plants. He reached out to clasp Jorie's outstretched fingers in one hand and Carrick's in the other. "From small seeds grow a great forest. From small dreams grow our race's greatest hope. And from your love will come the greatest gift we have to offer future generations: Two people become husband and wife, become father and mother... become partners, never to be apart." He joined their hands, clasping his palms over their interlaced fingers.

When Captain Andropolis pronounced her benediction, the words struck Jorie as more meaningful than she had thought they would be. "Jorie and Carrick, your children will be among the first to grow up on a new world. And their children will be born *on a planet,* not on a ship."

Jorie felt warm tears running down her cheeks. When the old man held up their hands and pronounced them married, the audience in the forest dome cheered.

With a mischievous smile, the Noah added, "My assistant Carrick has requested a small modification to personalize the ceremony. He assures me his new wife will understand the meaning."

Carrick had said nothing about this to her. Jorie shot him a glance. "What are you doing?"

"It's a blessing, like a baptism, to symbolize that we are going to put down roots on a new world at last." Carrick bent down to the edge of the narrow irrigation stream, scooped up a handful of the mud, and stood up. "Earth from Earth."

With an impish grin, he tossed the mud at her.

The audience members laughed. Jorie grabbed a handful and splatted it on Carrick's chest. "There," she said, "I suppose we belong together."

PART THREE

12

ANDRE PELLAR WAS MISERABLE, and it had nothing to do with the progress of the *Conquistador* Project. Questions and regrets swirled like a cyclone in his head. He could not concentrate on his real work. Thanks to the emotional turmoil, he made mistakes, forgot details, and brushed aside important double-checks. When one of the production lines stalled due to a misfiled requisition, Andre received a harsh official reprimand for his employee file, as well as an annoyed rebuke from Dr. Max (which stung him more than the reprimand did).

When quality-assurance teams discovered to their dismay that the integrated circuits monitoring the FTL distortion fields were flawed—one in ten had incorrect proton nesting—an entire batch had to be scrapped and re-manufactured, resulting in a three-day delay.

Dr. Max was furious. "This was on your watch, Andre! Why weren't you paying attention? The full-power test of the engines is in two days, and I will not miss that deadline!"

Andre hung his head. "I'm sorry, sir. It's…a personal matter."

"You don't have any *personal matters* that are more important than this project. Get your head back in your work." The physicist stalked off. While he was passionate about the *Con-*

quistador for its own sake, he hated even more to look bad in front of President Jurudu.

Andre turned back to the work, called up the overall flowchart screens, and studied delivery schedules for the highly volatile fuel components. The FTL engines had been constructed and were being loaded up for their first primary test. Despite the glitches, everything seemed back on track.

But Andre's thoughts kept drifting back to his argument with Renee, how she had shouted at him, begged him, and at the end, told him how disappointed she was.

All his life Andre had wanted nothing more than stability, a good home, regular meals. He worked hard and was pleased to have a few comforts that others didn't. He had no grandiose dreams, no aspirations to great power or fabulous wealth; he just wanted to do his job.

But Renee believed he could make a real difference, if only he would devote his mind to it, and she urged him to turn against the whole *Conquistador* Project. Although Andre sympathized with her point of view, and admired his distant cousins who had chosen to go aboard the *Beacon*, he did not see himself as a rebel.

Andre knew full well how carefully Jurudu's Surveillance & Security operatives monitored discussions, followed suspicious people. If any sabotage were to occur at Complex Alpha—as Renee seemed to want from him—Andre would never be able to hide his involvement. He couldn't believe she was naïve enough to ask such a thing, nor could he believe she would ever do more than talk, despite her vehemence.

Disappointed in his refusal, Renee lowered her expectations. If he refused to sabotage or hinder the project, then she begged him at the very least to take a moral stance, to walk away from further involvement. She wanted him to write a letter of resignation and defiantly hand it to Dr. Max Chambers-Osawa.

"How can I do that?" He had clenched his hands together, pleading with her. "Have you thought this through? How would I live? It wouldn't end there. President Jurudu would issue a Punitive Decree. I'd never get another job. I'd end up scraping out sewage-retention basins!"

Her dark eyes continued to flare as she watched him. He waited for her expression to soften, but it did not. He was accustomed to seeing love there, but now he saw only anger. "I'm glad everyone isn't so weak, Andre." The disgust was like acid in her voice. "If all the people aboard the *Beacon* had thought only of themselves, they never would have taken a gamble. There's more to being human than leading a comfortable life from day to day."

She packed up her possessions and left without a goodbye, without an apology, without giving him any reason for hope....

Around the expanded Complex Alpha, trucks and earth movers continued their round-the-clock work, and Andre buried himself in preparations for the full-power engine tests. After the FTL drives had been verified in private, behind the fences, Dr. Max would hold a formal public ceremony, during which he would fire up the engines in a grand and triumphant demonstration for President Jurudu, his generals, and all media cameras. First, however, Andre and Dr. Max had to make sure the basic engine systems worked; they would take no chances.

Flustered by Andre's lack of focus, Dr. Max had taken charge of the test preparations, insisting on watching every aspect. Andre was miserable to have his responsibility taken away, even temporarily, but that paled in comparison to his confusion and sadness over Renee. For the past four years, he had committed himself to his work, assuming he could have both the *Conquistador* Project and Renee. Contentment...was that so much for a hard-working man to earn?

He spent the next two days with an empty feeling in the pit of his stomach. The newly constructed FTL engine was scaled-up twice as large as the original probe engine. Dr. Max assumed the fuel-containment chambers would function as expected, but that had not yet been proved. Once the tests were passed, the President would give the green light to begin construction on the large ship itself. The FTL engines would be dismantled and delivered by heavy-lift launch vehicle up to orbit.

Eight years ago, Earth's launch capabilities had been used only for surveillance satellites and guardian weapons platforms but since Dr. Max's breakthrough, President Jurudu had revitalized the mothballed space program. Larger-scale orbital habitations, manufacturing yards, and space docks were well along the planning stages in preparation for building the *Conquistador*.

Dr. Max had been too preoccupied to consult with him all day long. Even though the physicist was upset with his poor recent job performance, Andre assumed that his presence would be mandatory at that evening's full-power test. If any results caused concerns, Andre might be needed to make last-minute refinements.

Two hours before the scheduled test, while he stared listlessly at delivery receipts, Andre received a direct voicecom message from Renee. On the screen, her image looked distraught, as if she'd been crying. Her voice sounded rough. "I need to see you. Meet me now—we've got to talk." She named a coffee club she often frequented.

He was elated to receive her call, to hear her voice. "Now? But I've got a major test in two hours. I have to be here when the engines—"

"Make your choice, Andre. That's what I asked all along. I need to see you tonight...or I don't need to see you at all. Maybe I misjudged you."

The words caught in his throat for an awkwardly long silence. Dr. Max had not officially asked him to be present at the test. In fact, he'd given Andre a cold shoulder. Andre tried to rationalize his decision, but he had already made up his mind. "I'm coming. I'll be there. In an hour?"

Her voice hitched. "Thank you, Andre."

He had barely enough time to race home, change into nice clothes, and stop by a vendor to purchase a wrapped bouquet of flowers. When he arrived at the coffee club, he felt nervous. It seemed like years since he had spoken with her or looked at her face.

When Renee saw him, her expression filled with love and...relief? She rose from the chair and gave him a silent hug. She whispered into his shoulder, "You came after all."

"I said I would."

They were on their second cup of coffee when the engine testing facility at Complex Alpha exploded, sending a geyser of fire halfway to orbit.

13

Jorie was five months pregnant when the accident happened to the *Beacon's* outer hull.

The *Beacon* had been cruising across space for 204 years. Having traveled through Earth's cometary cloud unscathed, they should have had smooth sailing in the far emptier regions between stars. Nevertheless, after so many years and such a vast distance, it was not statistically improbable that the course of the very large ship would intersect that of a very small rock.

The impact occurred during the ship's night cycle, and alarms awakened Jorie in her private quarters as well as Kora Andropolis in the Captain's cabin. Engineers were summoned to assess the damage. Bleary-eyed and edgy, Jorie hurried to the bridge.

Her belly was starting to show and she found herself walking differently, devoting an unusual amount of time to touching the curve of her abdomen. She noticed mood swings and hormonal changes (but often strenuously disagreed when Carrick pointed them out); it seemed as if some reckless and poorly trained pilot were guiding her internal biochemistry. She had already endured months of morning sickness, but the worst was not over—or so claimed her mother, Captain Andropolis, and any other mother she asked. She counted down the months until her baby was due.

When Jorie arrived on the bridge, Captain Andropolis was already looking at external-camera images of a torn furrow that extended across three hull plates.

"The good news—it could have struck at a worse spot," the Captain said. "Ten meters one way or the other, and the impact would have breached one of the stardrive reactor chambers. We wouldn't have survived the resulting explosion." She shook her head. "But it's still bad. The shielding is ruined in that section, and radiation from the reactor cell is leaking into space. That in itself doesn't give me any immediate heartburn, but it's also leaking down into the decks, and the impact is very close to the embryo storage vault and one section of our sperm bank."

Jorie understood the implications immediately. "That could cause genetic damage. We have to repair the shielding right away."

Andropolis turned to the concerned engineers gathered in the bridge. "See why I chose her as deputy?"

Jorie said, "We need to take a repair crew, suit up, and seal that leak."

"Not *we*, Jorie—I'll do it," Captain Andropolis said.

Jorie felt a flush of indignation. "I'm qualified!"

"You're also pregnant, and it's a radiation leak. I'll suit up and lead the team. In fact, I'm confident I could do the repairs myself, without risking anyone else."

"You need a backup, Captain," one of the engineers pointed out. "With the repair materials, it's a two-person job."

"All right, one backup—not a whole team. There's no need to expose everyone else."

"I should go," Jorie insisted, upset by the entire situation and trying to assert some form of control on it. She realized it was the hormones speaking, not her common sense.

"Do I need to remind you of your job title, Jorie?"

She raised her voice. "I'm Deputy Captain."

"Yes, and I'm *Captain*. That means the Deputy follows my orders. I'm well past my child-bearing years. The risk won't matter to me."

Jorie took two deep breaths and calmed herself, even though tears sprang to her eyes. She hated to be on this emotional roller-coaster. "I'm worried about you, Captain."

"Then that's a good job for you—stay here and worry while I go out and fix that breach. I've got to protect the sperm and egg bank and our entire genetic library."

Andropolis looked at the fidgeting engineers. "You there, choose who comes with me—draw straws or something. You've all been trained for this." She waved aside the two youngest men. "Neither of you are included."

Down in the equipment room and maintenance airlock bay, Captain Andropolis suited up, as did the chosen engineer. Jorie remained on the bridge, forced to serve as acting Captain until Andropolis came back aboard.

Frustrated and edgy, she used the *Beacon*'s external cameras to observe the two suited figures as they worked their way across the outer hull with repair kits and spare hull patches. Down below, a full engineering team donned radiation suits and worked their way through the interior decks to the reactor chambers, where they found the damage caused by the impact. From the inside, they erected temporary shielding to protect the genetic library.

Concerned, Jorie counted the seconds, knowing the radiation exposure the Captain and the engineer were facing. The spacesuits would give them some protection, but Jorie looked at the readings from the bridge monitoring screens, ran medical projections, and realized that both the Captain and the engineer had already received the maximum acceptable dosage.

Jorie called on the suit radio channel. "You should come back inside now. You're past the allowable limits. Send another team out."

"We're almost done, Jorie."

"You *are* done, Captain."

Andropolis ignored her. Twenty minutes later, the two of them finished up and came back inside through the airlock.

Jorie had summoned an emergency medical crew who rushed in with decontamination equipment, med checks, and monitoring devices. Jorie accompanied them, breathless. "We'll get you both to the infirmary, scan you, and give you our best pharmaceuticals to mitigate the exposure damage."

"We're *fine*." The Captain removed her helmet, tossed her short gray hair. "You worry too much—but don't come closer. There might be residual radiation on these suits."

Jorie did as she was told, but made sure the Captain listened as the doctors issued instructions. "I may only be Deputy Captain, but I have no desire to become Captain any sooner than absolutely necessary."

Andropolis gave her a wan smile. "Message received. Now please stop mothering me and take care of your own baby. I'll let the doctors do what they have to do."

14

After the explosions devastated Complex Alpha and ruined the FTL starship engine testbed, emergency crews swept in with the force of a massive military operation. President Jurudu imposed immediate martial law.

Leaving a distraught Renee at the coffee club, Andre raced back to the entry gates of the complex, where he was stopped by the army crackdown. It took him hours even to find someone who would admit to being in charge of the operation.

Amid the chaos, Andre could do nothing but stand there in the night and watch the columns of fire, unable to believe what he was seeing. He had meant to attend the test firing, but Renee had saved him! Otherwise, he would have been inside that inferno himself.

Dr. Max had certainly been there, but the Complex Alpha engine testbed was now nothing more than a large crater in the bright glow of a dying holocaust. Andre could hear the shouts of emergency crews, the crackle of flames. The broiling fumes in the air stung his eyes.

Andre couldn't imagine how such an accident had happened. Who had made such a grave miscalculation? He had studied and developed the engineering designs himself, and the FTL engines should have been stable, although the fuel supplies were, by their very nature, volatile.

No one would tell him if any survivors had been rescued, but he had no doubt that Dr. Max had vanished in the explosion.

✦

When Jurudu learned that Complex Alpha's chief administrator had survived the explosion without so much as a scratch, because he'd been conveniently offsite during the disaster, he summoned Andre to his Presidential palace. Immediately.

Without ceremony, security guards rounded him up from a holding area outside the blast zone. "Come with us, Dr. Pellar. The President wants to speak with you." He did not have the option to refuse.

Considering the investment the government had made in the *Conquistador* Project, and knowing the draconian measures Jurudu had imposed to maintain order since his coup, Andre was certain he would be brought up on charges of incompetence. Or executed without any charges at all.

Though the hour was late, all the lights burned in the Presidential palace. Additional soldiers were stationed at every entrance and the main windows. Surveillance flyers circled overhead, shining bright beams down on every possible approach to the building. The guards hustled him into Jurudu's private offices, and protocol soldiers stepped aside; everyone glared at Andre.

While Dr. Max had a rapport with the powerful leader, Andre was intimidated by Jurudu's presence. He had been in the President's office several times over the eight years of the project, but in each instance he had remained quiet, unobtrusive. In the day-to-day work at Complex Alpha, he did whatever was necessary to relieve Dr. Max of troublesome duties, without seeking glory or advancement for himself. Now, he expected President Jurudu would want to make an example of him.

Andre's face was smudged, his eyes red and irritated, his hair disheveled; he still wore the fine clothes he had donned for his meeting with Renee, and now they made him feel awkward. He wished he had on his laboratory jumpsuit with its Complex Alpha insignia.

Jurudu now rose from the sturdy chair behind his massive desk, looking like a thunderstorm contained within a business suit. "We are still assessing the damage, Dr. Pellar. For now, we believe that all has been lost—the test labs, the prototypes, the industrial facilities. Fortunately, we have backups of the plans in government archives."

"And…Dr. Chambers-Osawa?" A foolish question: No one could have survived such a terrible explosion. "Has there been any confirmation of—"

"He is dead. And you're not."

Andre hung his head, swallowing hard. "I don't know what could have happened, sir. I should have been there myself. I had a…personal emergency."

"We are aware of that, Dr. Pellar, and we're looking into it very carefully." Jurudu's brows furrowed. "Fortunately, the explosion occurred during your preliminary full-power test, rather than the formal running of the engines, which would have been heavily attended by high-level personnel. Including myself."

Andre felt cold inside. If the glitch had occurred later, not only would Dr. Max and Andre have been there, but the President, his generals, and countless industrial leaders as well.

"I must seize control of this setback," the President continued. "It was an accident, and we will not allow it to defeat us." He came around the desk to loom over Andre, assessing him. "Dr. Chambers-Osawa was the guiding force behind the *Conquistador* Project, but no man is indispensable. The responsibility now falls to you, Dr. Pellar. You understand the FTL plans. You grasp the workings of Complex Alpha." He set a massive hand on Andre's right shoulder. "Therefore, I am placing you in charge of both science and administration: Start from scratch, rebuild the facilities, recreate the blueprints and the technical teams from our security backups. Get us back on track—as swiftly as possible. The *Conquistador* must launch within the decade. We cannot lose to the *Beacon*."

Andre wiped at his burning cheeks. Some of the chemical smoke had irritated his skin. "It took us four years to reach this point, Mr. President. It'll take some time...."

The President regarded him with a steely gaze. "Take *less* than four years—I insist."

Andre knew better than to disagree. He tried to sound reassuring. "I will not let you down. This is a setback, yes, Mr. President—but not a defeat."

Jurudu shook Andre's hand in a crushing grip. "You will have everything you need...and I'll be watching you very closely."

Realizing the full import of the charge he'd just been given, Andre did not feel uplifted. Rather, it seemed as if a trapdoor had dropped open beneath his feet.

✦

Although he didn't feel like celebrating, he had to tell Renee the news. They had come close to resolving their differences in the coffee club, realizing (and admitting) how much they cared for each other. But now their personal crisis seemed trivial when compared with the disaster at Complex Alpha.

Overwhelmed by the responsibilities of his new position, he didn't get a chance to see her for two days. He was busy salvaging as much as possible from the ruins of Complex Alpha. The testing facilities were completely obliterated. Eight technicians had been killed, along with seventeen Surveillance & Security guards, and Dr. Max Chambers-Osawa.

He had no time to go home, had no opportunity for a quiet meal with Renee. It would be a long time before they could attempt to get their relationship back on a normal footing.

When they did finally get together, on the third day following the explosion, she hugged him, studying how haggard he looked. "I'm so sorry, Andre. It must have been a terrible blow. I know Dr. Max was your mentor, and he made so many opportunities possible for you, but you'll find another job. A man of your talents can do so many important things." She smiled at him, and her eyes were shining. "I've talked to my friends. Now that the *Conquistador* Project is over, we've got some ideas of big projects you could apply for."

"I already have a new job," he confessed. "A higher position."

She recoiled. "A higher position? What do you mean? I thought we decided—"

"The President named me the new director of the *Conquistador* Project. I know almost everything that Dr. Max did. We'll start over and build our own ship to Tau Ceti."

"Andre—you can't!"

Guilt gnawed at his heart, but he had made his decision. "If I don't accept the job, President Jurudu will find some other engineer to pore over the designs and begin the work again."

"You could have stalled," Renee said. "Didn't you think of all those people aboard the *Beacon*? Tau Ceti belongs to them. They earned it. If President Jurudu sends forces there, they'll take that new planet and...and turn it into another Earth. Look where we are now!"

The Surveillance & Security forces did not knock, nor did they show any courtesy when they scrambled the access plate on the door to Andre's apartment. They shouldered in two at a time until six heavily armed troops filled his main room. He was confused, but Renee retreated to the back of the room, frightened and furious at the same time.

The team sergeant stepped up. "Ms. Renee Sinha, we have orders to bring you with us. The Bureau has a few questions."

"Why would they want to talk to me?" she said.

Andre placed himself between her and the guards. "You can't just charge in here. I'm the Director of the *Conquistador* Project."

"We have an arrest warrant."

Andre snapped, "I'll call the President myself."

"This woman has been implicated in the terrorist bombings that destroyed the engine testbed and killed numerous people, including Dr. Chambers-Osawa."

Andre gaped at Renee, then turned his glare at the burly armed men. "Don't be ridiculous."

"Have a care, Dr. Pellar—we've also been looking into why you weren't present during the explosion. One might have expected you to be there."

"Are you suggesting that I am involved in some conspiracy? Ridiculous!"

The team sergeant remained stony-faced. "For the moment, we have no cause to arrest you, and the President himself commands you to continue your work without interruption. We have had constant surveillance monitors on your every move and have not yet found any suspicious activities. Ms. Sinha on the other hand...the dossier is not complete, but what we know is highly suspicious."

She fought, but they easily overpowered her. As the guards dragged Renee out of his apartment, Andre kept shouting, but to no effect. "Don't worry, I'll straighten this out," he called after her.

She gave him a defiant smile, but the guards pushed her along.

He never saw her again.

✦

When Andre tried to contact President Jurudu, he was dismayed to find that the administrative offices would not accept his calls. No one would tell him anything about Renee.

With so many repeated shocks—first the explosion, the death of Dr. Max, and now this, he could not concentrate on his work. He ignored his new responsibilities in the ruins of Complex Alpha, despite increasingly strident complaints from other workers, but he didn't care.

He made repeated calls, contacted government holding cells, worked his way up the chain of command in the Surveillance & Security Bureau, to no avail. Not only did they not let him speak to Renee or give him any update on her condition or the charges against her, they refused to acknowledge she was held prisoner at all.

Andre heard no reports in the news. There was no trial, no public outcry, despite the absurd allegations of terrorism laid against her. Officially, the explosion at Complex Alpha was determined to have been an unfortunate accident. Andre didn't know what to believe, although he supposed President Jurudu wouldn't want to acknowledge the rebels and would cover up any evidence of widespread unrest.

Finally, on his sixth urgent inquiry to the Presidential palace, the guards received permission to admit him. As soon as he entered the lavish office, he blurted out, "Mr. President, you must help me! The Bureau took my girlfriend, Renee Sinha. They haven't charged her—they've got no cause. I haven't been able to find her for two weeks."

Jurudu's hard face showed no sympathy. "I brought you here to refocus your mind on your true priorities, Dr. Pellar. That woman was taken into custody under my authority, and she has been handed over to the appropriate officials. That is no longer your business. The *Conquistador* Project is your business."

"At least let me see her. I've got to know that she's all right."

"No, Dr. Pellar, you do not. You can't afford any distractions, and so I am removing them from your life. There is so much work to do at Complex Alpha, and only thirteen years until the *Beacon* reaches Sarbras. You'd better get started."

PART FOUR

15

211 years since the Beacon's *departure from Earth.*
6 years to scheduled arrival at Tau Ceti.

THE *BEACON* FLEW ONWARD, growing ever closer to Tau Ceti. But with only six years remaining in their voyage, the hopeful colonists were stunned by the unexpected news from Earth.

When President Jurudu's transmission arrived, Jorie was giving Captain Andropolis the weekly report; they watched the message as if it were some kind of outdated entertainment loop. More than a decade out of date, the broadcast could not possibly have any relevance to them aboard the *Beacon*. Separated by such an inconceivable distance, Earth seemed less real to Jorie than Sarbras did. From the ship's observation windows, she could see the bright yellow-orange of Tau Ceti much more clearly than she could find the faint third-magnitude speck of Earth's sun, far back in their past.

When the blustery President appeared on the image screen, Andropolis let out a rude snort. "I'm surprised he's still around."

"This is a special message to the colonists and crewmembers aboard the generation ship *Beacon*: The human race is resilient, and our planet has recovered from its most difficult times. Through my leadership, we have fostered an ambitious program of scientific research—and that vision has borne fruit. Our greatest physicists have discovered a new means of spacecraft propulsion, a faster-than-light drive that can propel one of our ships to Tau Ceti in only a few months' time.

"My chief scientist, Dr. Max Chambers-Osawa, is spearheading this effort, the most ambitious new project Earth has undertaken since the *Beacon*. We are in the process of designing and testing these engines, after which we will build our own colony ship. A project of this scope requires hard work and sacrifice from every citizen, but we choose to dedicate ourselves to this demonstration of human persistence and ingenuity.

"Due to the transmission delay, you will not hear my words for more than a decade. By that time, we expect our own Sarbras colony will already be established and thriving." Jurudu smiled, flashing white teeth with an air of smug superiority. "When you finally arrive, we will help you integrate into our existing settlement."

After the message ended, Jorie sat in stunned silence, just staring at the bulkhead wall. She felt sick inside. "We've spent more than two hundred years on this journey. Our parents and grandparents and great-grandparents died for this dream!"

"No, Jorie—they *lived* for this dream." Captain Andropolis was gray, trembling, but she summoned her courage. "We will still get to Sarbras. Nothing can stop us."

Jorie tried to draw strength from the Captain's words, but she knew that when the *Beacon* passengers heard this, they would be devastated and outraged. Jorie had promised her own two children—Burton and Carrie, ages seven and four—a wonderful new life once they reached Sarbras. She had to wonder what sort of people President Jurudu would send there to plant his flag; the man clearly meant to conquer, rather than cooperate.

"That message is out of date," Andropolis pointed out. "By now, they've already done whatever they intended to do, or they failed in the attempt. Nothing we can do about it from here. But bear in mind that regimes like Jurudu's don't tend to last long. Given the hardships inherent in such a project, maybe he was overthrown before his FTL ship launched. We can always hope."

Jorie tried to maintain her optimism. "We have a few thousand people here aboard the *Beacon*. Even if Earth sends another colony ship the same size, isn't a planet big enough for all of us?"

Andropolis let out a bitter laugh. "Earth wasn't."

They discussed, but only briefly, withholding the news from the rest of the colonists, but Andropolis said, "We can't keep it from our people. That isn't who we are."

"We have to tell the crew together, Captain," Jorie said. "We have to show everyone aboard the *Beacon* that there is hope."

"We're good at clinging to hope. That's what we do best." The old woman gave her a comforting pat on the shoulder. "We'll let everyone digest the message from President Jurudu, and then we'll hold an all-hands meeting to discuss the matter and look at solutions."

16

AFTER SEVEN YEARS OF CONSTRUCTION work, the *Conquistador* was finally taking shape. The framework and half-finished hull looked magnificent in the images sent down from the orbiting shipyard. Andre took pride in that at least.

The labor had consumed his life; thanks to President Jurudu, he had nothing else to live for.

After the disastrous testbed explosions and the death of Dr. Max, Andre rebuilt the vital facilities at Complex Alpha in a year. He gathered a new team to reconstruct the basic work of the *Conquistador* and the FTL engines. Andre was adamant: The industrial construction work for the starship engines, as well as the body of the colony ship in orbit, operated under the most stringent of safety protocols. Delicate calculations were triple-checked. No chance for error, no more disasters.

Still ruling Earth after more than sixteen years, President Jurudu watched the clock ticking and the project's expenses mounting. Though the President was dissatisfied, Andre had only to say, "I can rush ahead and cut corners, sir, if you'd like me to increase the chances of another accident happening."

Jurudu increased security instead. Both men knew that, contrary to official reports, the previous explosion had been no accident.

No matter how much the President pushed him, Andre could not feel the sense of urgency; in fact, he did not feel much at all. With Renee gone forever, he was a hollow man shackled to his duties, and he could not summon any enthusiasm for the *Conquistador* to match the passion Renee and her friends had had for stopping it.

Andre had never seen her after the Surveillance & Security troops seized her in his apartment, and finally he had learned not to ask further questions. But that did not stop him from wondering and grieving.

Plodding through his duties, he managed to see the *Conquistador* finished. Stage after stage, he had modeled his work on the construction of the *Beacon* two centuries earlier. That goal seemed so much purer. During the time of solar flares and climate upheavals, people had accepted the need for desperate measures; they pulled together, worked hard, sacrificed resources, making the necessary gamble on the generation ship.

Now, however, the people of Earth did not have the same determination or sense of urgency. The reason for such an effort was not clear to them. The *Conquistador* was President Jurudu's singular obsession, and he held the power to make it happen, despite public opinion. He ignored the fact that the massive FTL project drained the treasury almost as much as had the earlier Tau Ceti project, which he so often ridiculed and reviled.

The bulk of the vessel's assembly work occurred at new industrial stations in orbit, which drifted alongside observation platforms and satellite weapons emplacements that helped

Jurudu maintain his control on Earth. Andre, however, spent most of his time with his feet on the ground working inside Complex Alpha, which had now grown to enormous size.

The rebuilt full-sized FTL engines had been tested and installed in the ship framework, and were guarded every moment against sabotage. Each orbital construction worker went through the most rigorous security checks, and their family members were monitored or even kept under house arrest as a guarantee of loyalty.

When Andre asked to be reassigned, Jurudu would hear none of it. "This project is yours, Dr. Pellar—not just the FTL engine design and testing, not just the orbital assembly of the vessel. All of it. See it through! I need you to make the *Conquistador* a true colony ship, choose the right people, the right supplies, and the right equipment so that the thousand brave colonists can set up a thriving new outpost on Sarbras."

Andre frowned, considering the magnitude of the request. He could find the old manifests for equipment and supplies that the *Beacon* planners had chosen, but select all the colonists as well? "That will require a lot of research, sir. I'll need access to all possible technical, government, and library records I might require."

"Yes, yes. I will arrange it." Andre knew Jurudu would insist on vetting each one of them for loyalty, but the President was also anxious for the ship to launch.

Andre drew a deep breath, tried to summon a semblance of enthusiasm. "I'll get to work, then. Our estimated completion date is four years."

"Make it three years. We have waited too long already."

Andre knew that was patently unrealistic. "I will do my best, sir."

✦

A blustery red-headed officer presented himself to Andre in the Complex Alpha administrative barracks. He was short in stature, barely five foot three inches, but his ego made him seem taller—at least the officer appeared to think so. His dark uniform showed he was from the Surveillance & Security Bureau rather than the military or police forces. The lower part of his uniform blouse was buttoned tightly over a slight paunch.

"Dr. Pellar, I am Commander Karl Vinton, and I wanted to express my congratulations. I have long studied your work. President Jurudu speaks very highly of your abilities, and he insisted that we meet face-to-face, since we'll be spending so much time together."

Andre was already sure he didn't like whatever this small red-headed officer was about to tell him. "Congratulations for what, Commander?"

Vinton flushed. "On being selected the prime civilian contact aboard the *Conquistador*. You'll be the highest ranking civilian on the ship when it heads for Tau Ceti."

"*On* the ship? I'm going along?"

"Yes, President Jurudu requested it, and I am the expedition's commander. It's already been decided."

Andre had to sit down. "I'm leaving Earth? I did not request—"

"It's a great honor, surely you won't dispute that. After devoting your life to the *Conquistador*, it's only fitting that you go along to make certain that nothing goes wrong."

His thoughts spun. Perhaps Jurudu was trying to get rid of him, or to make sure that Andre himself didn't attempt any sabotage?

Vinton continued, "In the first years of setting up our initial base on Sarbras, no doubt I will often rely on your expertise. The President has charged me to administer the base, fly his flag, and hold Sarbras in his name."

Andre tried to speak, but no words came out at first. Finally, he said, "You'll have others to rely on besides myself, Commander. The President has tasked me with selecting the most qualified colonists, experts in numerous disciplines so that we can establish a self-sustaining settlement."

Vinton paced the barracks room. "Don't forget that these experts must also show proven loyalty to President Jurudu."

Andre said, "Everyone is loyal to President Jurudu."

"That goes without saying, but we have to make sure." The redheaded officer turned to face him. "Now then, tell me the truth—exactly how soon can we depart?"

"The scheduled launch date is four years from now, Commander."

"I know, I know, but when can we really depart? Everyone pads their estimates."

"Four years, Commander," Andre said. "We cannot be careless. Once we head out of the solar system, we won't be able to turn around and come back home because somebody forgot a pair of sunglasses."

Vinton grimaced. He seemed to be a man who lost his temper easily. "There's nothing frivolous about this, Dr. Pellar."

"I'm not being frivolous. We'll have a thousand people aboard, and they will be the seeds of our colony. Even though the duration of our FTL voyage will be only two months instead of two centuries, we need to bring enough materials for us to survive until we can establish our colony. We'll need greenhouses, seeds, livestock, medical supplies, and raw materials for...everything."

"Keep it to the basics, Dr. Pellar. Our people are accustomed to austerity—we'll get by." Vinton turned to take his leave, and then glanced over his shoulder as he paused by the door. "Besides, we can take anything else we need from the storehouses aboard the *Beacon* as soon as they arrive. After all, everything they have belongs to the people of Earth. Therefore, it's ours."

17

ONCE THE COLONISTS ABOARD the *Beacon* heard the message from Earth, some felt betrayed, others were confused or despairing. By turns, they imagined doomsday scenarios or hopeful dreams of sharing resources and forming a united Sarbras colony better than would have been possible before.

The one bright spot in the otherwise startling message was a large dataset appended—perhaps surreptitiously—to the end of Jurudu's speech: complete results from the initial FTL probe to Tau Ceti, with better detail on Sarbras than the *Beacon*'s best long-distance telescopes could obtain.

The probe data also proved that Earth did indeed have the capability to send a ship at speeds faster than light.

Jorie reviewed the probe information with the team of planetary scientists who had studied all available data about Sarbras. "At any other point in our journey, these probe images would have been the most exciting news we could imagine," she admitted. "Now it's just part of a new problem we're going to face."

"We'll study it anyway, Deputy Captain," said one of the planetary scientists. "On the positive side, the data verifies our projections. The planet does appear to be habitable."

"Good, one problem solved at least. Maybe we can figure out the rest during our all-hands meeting."

✦

Captain Andropolis and the Noah stood together facing the audience, as many people as could crowd inside the forest dome; the discussion was also broadcast to the three thousand crewmember-colonists via public screens.

The Noah looked the same as always, silver-haired and beatific. As Deputy Captain, Jorie waited behind them, ready to have her own say.

Andropolis opened the meeting. "Today, we discuss the destiny of the *Beacon*. You've all heard the message Earth transmitted. A faster ship may have already reached Sarbras and established a separate colony there. Still, we don't know what's happened on Earth in the past eleven years—whether President Jurudu remained in power, whether he succeeded in pushing through his gigantic FTL project, or whether it even worked. We simply don't know—and so we can't plan for it. We can only discuss hypotheticals."

She turned to Jorie, who picked up the discussion with a firm voice, not alarmist, but realistic. "The tone of Jurudu's message was clear, and it did not sound peaceful. If Earth sent a new mission to Tau Ceti that arrived at Sarbras well ahead of us, I suspect they'll want to conquer the planet for themselves, not hold it as stewards of humanity."

She looked around the audience, feeling a knot in her stomach. "However, at least we have fair warning, and we have time to prepare. During our long voyage, no one thought we would need weapons, but we can no longer be so naïve. We have the scientific knowledge. We could retool some of our equipment to be used as weaponry—*defensive* weaponry. Better to have the weapons and not need them, than to be caught weak and unprepared."

She was troubled by what she was proposing. She looked at the audience gathered under the tall birch trees; Carrick was there, watching their two children, holding them. She glanced at them, smiled, then squared her shoulders. "We have to prepare to defend ourselves and assert our rights to Sarbras—*our* planet." Uneasy murmurs swept through the audience.

The Noah sounded alarmed and shaky. "You're talking about war. My forebears did not give up everything and fly away just to bring Earth conflicts to some other solar system. There is another possibility."

He paused for a long moment, as if uncertain whether to voice his suggestion. "The *Beacon* has traveled for 211 years, and we've done just fine for ourselves. Gathering hydrogen between the stars, we have all the energy we need. Instead of running low on fuel supplies after such a long journey, we actually have a surplus—and I see no reason why that would change."

The old man looked around the audience. "Why can't we just continue our voyage? Bypass Tau Ceti entirely, have our astronomers search for another star with another planetary system, and then head there? Maybe it'll take us another two centuries or longer, but that planet will be ours. We won't have to fight for it."

From the grumbling in the audience, Jorie could tell that most rejected the idea of extending their voyage endlessly. Andropolis said, "If Earth has faster-than-light ships, they may well spread out to all other habitable planets well before we can get there."

"We will try to come to a peaceful resolution, but sometimes you have to take a stand," Jorie said. "True, our ancestors didn't imagine the possibility of war, but what would they think if we simply gave up and ran from any hope of finding a home?"

Hearing the mutters from the audience, the Captain stepped forward and spoke in her calm, maternal voice. "Now that we are close, we have a much better estimate of our arrival time at Tau Ceti. Throughout this long voyage, the engineers have maintained our stardrive, conserved fuel, improved the engine efficiency. We're just now entering the dusty fringes of the Tau Ceti system, and our ramscoop has harvested even more hydrogen than we had planned on. Even if we do nothing else, we are due to arrive at Sarbras three months sooner than originally expected." She waited, listening to happy gasps around the audience.

"And that's if we *do nothing*," Andropolis continued. "We've always been careful and conservative—that's how we survived so successfully. We kept the surplus of fuel as a vital reserve. We've never needed it before. Now, however, given the new and uncertain situation, I propose that we use the fuel to *accelerate*. We can make a last push toward the finish line and arrive at Tau Ceti nine months to a year before the projected date." The Captain paused to let that sink in, then added in a grimmer voice, "A year sooner than anyone from Earth can possibly expect us to arrive. We can surprise them."

Captain Andropolis sealed the deal by saying, "I do not like the prospect of conflict—we will avoid it, if at all possible—but I am not prepared to surrender our dreams and run away from Sarbras because we might face a few difficulties.

We all knew we'd encounter challenges. We can't keep going forever. We have to stay the course, get to our new world… and then trust in our common humanity."

✦

After the meeting, the Captain asked Jorie to join her in her private quarters. Jorie felt unsettled but oddly energized by the decision. They had so much work to do—accelerating the ship, reassessing their reserves, studying bargaining strategies, and developing ways to defend the *Beacon*, if needed. Fortunately, they had several years to get it all done.

In the decade and a half since Captain Andropolis chose her as deputy, Jorie had gradually assumed more and more of the Captain's duties, especially recently. Andropolis joked that she was getting old and deserved a bit of relaxation. Jorie could tell that the Captain's health was waning, so she tried harder to shoulder responsibilities, meet with the crew, and go outside on the regular inspection expeditions of the slow-ship's hull.

Now Andropolis sat on her narrow bed and smiled, though she looked very tired, as if the recent decision had drained her. "An excellent performance, Jorie. Well done."

"I'm already feeling overwhelmed, but I know everyone will pull together."

The Captain nodded slowly. "I wanted to wait until after the meeting to tell you. *You* are the one who has to be strongest now, because there's something else…." The old woman absently rubbed her left breast, leaned back with a weary sigh. "The doctors found something. They can't remove it, but they've been treating me for the past month. It's going to get much worse, but I'll fight it."

Jorie looked at the Captain, even more stunned than by President Jurudu's transmission from Earth.

"I'm not worried." Captain Andropolis gave a brave smile. "I know that I picked the best Deputy Captain."

PART FIVE

18

215 years since the Beacon's *departure from Earth.*
2 years to originally scheduled arrival at Tau Ceti.

FINALLY, ALMOST TWO DECADES AFTER Dr. Max's discovery of the faster-than-light drive, the *Conquistador* was ready to depart for the nearest sun-like star—Tau Ceti, 11.9 light years away.

The last day he breathed the air of Earth, Andre Pellar gazed across the landscape and tried to imagine Earth's former beauty...but he saw only the fenced-in industrial Complex Alpha. He had expected to feel more regret—after all, he was flying away and would not be coming back. Why did it not make him sad to turn his back on everything?

He decided that what he would miss most was the *dream* of Earth. The imaginary stories—some records called it "history"—of how beautiful this world had once been, although Andre had never seen it that way.

He had packed his possessions, but found little he wanted to take with him. Most of his life had been spent chained to the *Conquistador* Project, and now he would be riding aboard the colony ship he had constructed. What other keepsakes did he need?

He did find three old letters that Renee had written him, a scrap of a grocery list in her handwriting, and a pair of earrings he had bought for her, which she'd worn only once, claiming they were too extravagant. He even kept a small envelope that contained a few strands of her hair from a brush in the apartment's bathroom. It had been an ancient tradition for sailors to carry a lock of their sweetheart's hair when they embarked on a long voyage; Andre thought he was being silly and sentimental, but he brought the strands along anyway. They weighed almost nothing, yet they made his heart heavy.

Now, as he looked at the blue-green world dwindling in the rear sensor screens as the *Conquistador* headed out of Earth orbit, Andre's sense of loss was only theoretical. Renee had already been gone for more than a decade, and he had survived that pain.

His greatest happiness, he realized far too late, had been his time with her. But he had sacrificed that happy partnership by joining Dr. Max on a project that gave a sense of being important…but it was only an illusion. If he had let himself be satisfied with a more mundane job, maybe he and Renee would still be together.

She was long lost to him, locked away in a gulag somewhere, enslaved in a horrific mine, or perhaps (mercifully?) dead. Gone was gone…and now Andre would be gone, along with the thousand others aboard the *Conquistador*.

✦

During the final preparatory month, he had smiled through—but was immune to—the delirious departure celebrations and President Jurudu's grand speeches. Commander Karl Vinton thrived in his position, making grandiose public promises to the President, swearing that the *Conquistador* would carry the torch of human civilization into the darkness of the universe, that he would lay down the first stepping stone to the stars. The metaphors seemed endless, and Vinton's pompous promises were so vehement that even Jurudu grew visibly impatient with him. The Commander was definitely cast from the same mold as President Jurudu, with an added dash of Napoleonic hubris.

However, in the months before departure, Andre had grown to like the *Conquistador*'s assigned second in command,

Major Sendy Montoir. She was in her early thirties and had been chosen for her intelligence, her cooperation, and her track record of government service, not to mention her biological fitness and ranking on the breeding index.

Every one of the thousand crewmembers aboard the FTL ship had passed rigorous health scans. Some of the best candidates Andre put forward during the crew-selection process were disqualified because of infertility or troublesome genetic markers. Andre understood the necessity of that, and he even received strict instructions to take a mate of his own and have offspring in order to expand the colony as soon as they were settled on Sarbras.

The thought only made him regret that he and Renee never had the opportunity to have a family. He wasn't sure he deserved to have a second chance....

After the *Conquistador* had passed beyond the Earth-Moon system, Andre made his way to the bridge for the official activation of the FTL engines. He'd reviewed and tweaked the calculations so many times over the past few years that he knew every detail by heart, could see no possible chance for error. Even so, the FTL hadn't been tested with passengers aboard. Would the human body, or mind, endure the transition to faster-than-light speeds, outside the realm of traditional physics? What effects might it have on consciousness?

They were gambling everything on this. President Jurudu had demanded it.

Though originally designed by Dr. Max, the faster-than-light engines had become Andre's private project. Standing on the *Conquistador*'s bridge, he assumed that he would have the ceremonial honor of activating the FTL and plunging the ship into its headlong flight to Tau Ceti. Finishing the job.

Commander Vinton, however, insisted on doing it himself. Andre did not make an issue of it, but he did view the detail as a measure of Vinton's character. From her station on the other side of the bridge, First Officer Montoir swiveled in her chair and glanced at Andre. An understanding flashed between them, but Andre just shrugged.

With a grandiose gesture, Commander Vinton gestured forward, as if announcing the start of a great race. "Onward, to Tau Ceti!"

The faster-than-light engines activated, and acceleration shifted the *Conquistador*. The stars blurred, and then the sensor screens went gray and blank. They were flying blind.

The Commander lurched up from his seat. "What is this? A malfunction?"

Andre explained, "No, sir. Our velocity is greater than the speed of light." He waited a moment, saw no understanding on Vinton's face. "We're traveling faster than any signal can be received by our sensors, sir. We've left the electromagnetic spectrum behind."

He went over to the control modules, studied the engine diagnostics, and nodded. "Rest assured, sir, the FTL is functioning exactly as expected. We should already be approaching the boundaries of the Earth's solar system." He grinned with pride, despite himself. "The *Beacon* took fifteen years to get this far."

This, Commander Vinton understood. Satisfied, he gave a brisk nod. "Good work, Dr. Pellar. President Jurudu would be proud."

✦

During the first week of the voyage, First Officer Montoir became the public face of command, more personable than the red-headed Vinton. She walked among the personnel, delivering directives from the Commander, who remained in his offices where he could write grand plans. Now that the *Conquistador* was forever separated from Earth, he seemed to consider himself far more important than before.

Vinton issued directives listing alternatives for the colony depending on landforms, climate, and the accessibility of mineral deposits. He drew up complex response plans to deal with any problems the *Beacon* might pose whenever it arrived. These documents read like President Jurudu's detailed austerity plans, but Andre recognized that they were complete fabrications. No one knew what to expect on Sarbras. Nevertheless, Commander Vinton insisted that everyone read his white papers, and he had one of his big-shouldered lockstep officers, Major Wexler, distribute them to all crewmembers; few of the colonists took the papers seriously.

Two weeks into the voyage, the Commander instituted a daily briefing with Andre and First Officer Montoir to discuss their arrival plan. Sometimes, Major Wexler sat in on the meetings, but rarely spoke.

Using enhanced (and fabricated) probe images, Vinton had selected several possible locations for their first colony settlements, including likely areas for large-scale mining excavations. Andre cautioned him. "Commander, I studied those images myself as well as the raw data. The manipulations and enhancements are...questionable. I would place little confidence in their accuracy."

Vinton was troubled. "These were officially released by the President's office."

"They were designed for propaganda purposes, sir," said First Officer Montoir. "Consider them a best-case scenario. Realistically, what we find may not match those rosy pictures."

"I prefer to put my faith in the President's analysis and data," said Wexler, "until we are given a reason to do otherwise."

Andre did not remind the man that *he* and Dr. Max had been responsible for the probe data, not President Jurudu.

Frowning, Vinton put the images aside. "Very well, then, our plans can be flexible. According to projections, we will arrive up to two years before the *Beacon* shows up. Plenty of time."

"Again, sir," Andre cautioned, "there's a fair amount of uncertainty in that number. We don't know the *Beacon*'s precise velocity. Even a tiny discrepancy either way could add up to years. And the *Conquistador* itself is likely to require course correction once we arrive in the Tau Ceti system."

Growing angry, Vinton said, "You scientists are like law-yers, unwilling to say anything with certainty! I need concrete data in order to make plans. We're not just setting up a camp-site—this is a military operation. We have orders to seize and hold an entire planet."

"I thought we were building a colony," Sendy Montoir said.

"We're establishing a *beachhead*, a base of operations."

"I'll go back to my offices and review the information, Commander." Andre backed away. "Before we left, I copied all of the scientific, historical, and governmental databases. We possess two hundred years of information gathering and analysis beyond anything the *Beacon* had."

He did not point out that the scientists aboard the old generation ship had also had two centuries to make improve-ments and new discoveries.

"I'll give you the most precise data we have, sir."

"Good work, Dr. Pellar," Vinton said. "Don't let me down."

✦

In his last few months on Earth, Andre had assembled countless classified databases and loaded them into his pass-word-protected library system aboard the *Conquistador*. He considered this concession from the President to be a coup as great as when Jurudu had overthrown the squabbling war-lords who ruled before him. The President didn't even grasp the significance of what his project manager had done; Andre had everything he needed.

"Information is the foundation of our civilization, Mr. President," he had told Jurudu, looking earnest and innocent. "I request your permission to copy all scientific and histori-cal records into the *Conquistador*'s computers. In fact, since we are establishing a new foothold for humanity, let us bring all cultural artifacts as well—government documents, census records, the complete annals of your Presidency, classified and unclassified. Everything."

Jurudu had frowned. "How can all those things be relevant?"

"We are traveling into the unknown, Mr. President—I can't begin to guess what might or might not be useful. We have the capacity to store everything, so why shouldn't we bring all those records? Besides, think of it as a backup. What if a later administration tried to rewrite everything you did? It wouldn't matter, because we'll have the original records, undoctored, for posterity. We will carry the accurate records to Sarbras—they will be your legacy on a new world."

"Part of my legacy." Jurudu touched his chin with an extended finger and nodded slowly. "We have to think in the long term."

Andre added his last point. "On the other hand, if you wish me to develop a specific list of topics that are most likely to be useful, that will take some time. How can I possibly foresee everything we might need? We know very little about Sarbras, so I recommend we err on the side of comprehensiveness. And even if I did identify all the necessary information, it would take more time to select millions of specific files from Earth's databases than just to copy everything. We might not make our launch date."

"Very well, I see your point. Do what you need to do—but make certain it happens quickly. I don't want to delay the departure of the *Conquistador* by a single hour."

Andre copied all of the databases, including encrypted and classified government records. Although some security librarians were skeptical, he showed them the President's direct authorization; when they double-checked the authorization, they received a terse command to "do what Dr. Pellar asks." And so Andre took everything.

Everything.

Now in his quarters aboard the FTL ship, instead of compiling improbable data as Commander Vinton asked, Andre continued decrypting the deep interrogation files, poring over years of grim records kept by the Surveillance & Security Bureau.

It took him two days, but finally—finally—he found the full report on Renee Sinha.

19

Since her cancer diagnosis, Captain Andropolis kept out of the public eye as much as possible. Four years of treatments seemed to be tearing her apart from within; she looked gaunt and emaciated, her hair had fallen out, and her voice trembled.

The *Beacon*'s medical department had kept the Captain's condition secret for as long as possible—nearly a full year—giving Andropolis the freedom to reveal the news when she decided the time was right. However, the ship's Captain was such a prominent figure that her absence was noted, and whenever she was seen in public, the signs of her struggle were unmistakable for anyone who bothered to look.

The crewmember-colonists drew their own conclusions well before Andropolis made her announcement in a ship-wide speech. They were saddened, but they dealt with the news, as they had done so many times before.

Jorie took on more duties, meeting the Captain daily for conversation and a cup of tea in her bridge office. "You never should have gone outside to repair the hull damage and the radiation leak," she scolded her. "You stayed out too long. You should have listened to me and sent repair teams out in shifts."

"All those years ago? You're making assumptions. We can't know the cause of my cancer," Andropolis said. "Maybe it was something I ate."

The doctors also monitored the engineer who had gone outside with the Captain after the meteoroid impact, running repeated tests. Although Andropolis suffered from a deadly lymphoma, the engineer remained completely healthy. The older woman accepted the situation. "The embryo library and sperm bank are safe, so I consider it a fair exchange."

Jorie tried to tell herself that the Captain's condition was only deteriorating as a result of the harsh medical treatments. She pretended that the worst would soon be over and Andropolis would regain her strength. Before long, she would be the same powerful and determined Captain that Jorie had served for more than half of her life.

Andropolis gave her a maternal smile. "I've always loved you for your optimism, young lady, but we both know that simply won't be the case. I've fought this for four years, but the prognosis is not good. I can put on a brave face and make my farewell announcement. Soon enough I won't be fit to lead this ship."

Tears welled in Jorie's eyes. "But you can't die yet! We're only a little more than a year out, thanks to our acceleration. You have to stay alive long enough to see Sarbras. Just hold on until you can set foot on our new world. Don't you want to be buried in real soil?"

"No, send me out like the other Captains before me. I want to continue my voyage."

✦

For her farewell address to the *Beacon*, Captain Andropolis looked surprisingly strong and energetic, and Jorie knew she had taken stimulants and supplements to make this public appearance. The doctors warned her against stressing her system too much, but Andropolis had insisted. "I can't just think of myself. We have higher priorities."

Gaunt, her skin hanging loose on her bones, she called the meeting to order and addressed the obvious issue head-on. "This will be my last meeting as your official Captain. Some might say it's because my health is declining, but there's more to it. I know that Jorie Platt can do a better job than I, especially in these times of turmoil as we arrive. While you all figure out what to do with the other Earth colonists, if they even made it to Sarbras, I'd prefer to relax in retirement." When she chuckled, a few others added polite laughs, but most of the listeners remained awkwardly silent.

Jorie stood beside her mentor, stoic, shedding no tears. Kora Andropolis had survived much longer than their initial estimates, but the doctors were certain that she had less than six months now, probably closer to three.

"My life is just one life—and it is mine. And I do what I choose with it," Andropolis said. "I give you your new Captain." She took Jorie's hand, raised it high. "She'll take you the rest of the way to Sarbras."

2 0

THE *CONQUISTADOR*'S FTL DRIVE shut down at the calculated time, and the ship began its extreme deceleration back below lightspeed. On the bridge, Andre drew in deep breaths, trying to loosen the knot in his stomach. The moment of truth.

Upon arriving at the new star system, he would accept credit for success…but knew he would receive a dressing down from Commander Vinton if anything went wrong. The Commander himself stood in his finest (though no longer relevant) uniform, full of decorations from his service in the Surveillance & Security Bureau before he was promoted and assigned to the *Conquistador* Project.

During the two months of passage, Andre had gone from disliking the man to truly despising him, but he kept his feelings hidden—a skill he had learned working under President Jurudu's administration.

As soon as the FTL engines shut down, the red-headed Commander looked ready to declare victory. Lording it over his underlings, he looked like a short-statured bully. Half an hour later, the screens remained gray, and Vinton grew impatient. "What's taking so long? Are we lost?"

"We're decelerating, sir," Andre explained, "but the ship is still moving faster than light. Soon enough, we'll drop below the threshold, and our sensors will function again."

Three hours later, they received the first glimpse of their new surroundings, with Tau Ceti shining bright and golden in the distance. The navigators took images of the star field, logged Tau Ceti's relative coordinates, and calculated the ship's exact position.

"Where is our planet?" Vinton asked, rubbing his temples. "Shouldn't it be right in front of us?"

Andre fought back a scowl at the man's stupidity. "It's not easy to spot a planet in an open starfield, sir. We traveled nearly twelve light years—you can't expect us to appear right in orbit over the planet."

Once the navigation experts determined the angle of the ecliptic, they began their search for planetary bodies in earnest. By late that evening, they did locate Sarbras. The *Conquistador* had arrived on the far fringe of the Tau Ceti system, and the habitable world was on the opposite side of the sun.

"We overshot the target," Andre said. "We're approximately 1.2 billion kilometers from the planet. With standard engines, it'll take about eight weeks to make our way there. No cause for concern; we have sufficient fuel and supplies."

"We're still *two months* away? How did this happen?" The Commander looked at Andre, then at First Officer Montoir. "Was there a miscalculation? Was there a malfunction in your FTL engines? How could such a grave error occur?"

Unfortunately, Andre was not ready to confront the man, present his evidence, and take the necessary action. Not yet. He counted to three, calmed himself. "Commander, let me clarify for you." He did not entirely succeed in keeping the impatient tone from his voice. "We traveled *11.9 light years*—over a hundred trillion kilometers—and missed our destination by only a little more than a billion kilometers. An error of less than one ten-thousandth of one percent...with a technology that has never been used once in the field at full scale. That is amazing accuracy, sir."

He held the Commander's glare for a long moment, before adding, "I expected this, and we'll fix it. But we're here for the long-haul. A permanent colony. What does eight weeks matter?"

Vinton was flustered and shifted his attention elsewhere. He looked queasy, as if he suffered from a sudden bout of space sickness. "Is there any sign of the *Beacon*? Do you see their ship in the system? Any indication of settlements on the planet?"

"We're too far from Sarbras to detect settlements, sir, but a vessel the size of the generation ship would be prominent now if it were in orbit. They haven't arrived yet."

"At least that's worked to our advantage," Vinton said. "Make certain the *Conquistador* is visible so they can see us and be afraid."

Andre bit back a sharp retort. Clearly, Commander Vinton had no idea of the size of the *Beacon*.

"No question that they'll see us when they arrive, Commander," said First Officer Montoir. "In the meantime we can scan Sarbras with our high-res imagers. That will let us plan our colony. By the time we arrive, we'll be ready to dispatch our prefab units and set up groundside industries."

Vinton grumbled, but didn't argue. "Set course for the planet. I want to get moving as soon as possible."

✦

With high-resolution scans, they were finally able to compile reasonable maps of Sarbras. They found oceans, land, and weather systems. The atmosphere showed the right levels of breathable gases. The continents looked habitable, covered with vegetation.

Part of one landmass was tectonically active with a field of angry volcanoes that sent lava plumes so high into the atmosphere that they were visible from the other side of the solar system, but the other continents appeared to be unaffected. Off at sea, a gigantic hurricane system formed a vortex of clouds—very rough weather, but Andre remembered the years of terrible climate upheavals on Earth during the heaviest solar flares. It was nothing they couldn't tolerate.

All in all, the preliminary results left Andre optimistic. The greatest danger wasn't the planet Sarbras, but Commander Vinton and the corrupt baggage he brought from Earth.

As for the crew aboard the ship, a significant number suffered from the onset of migraines, queasiness, and a general feeling of unsettled aches. Andre himself felt fine, and the medical department could find no specific reason for the reported illnesses. Andre thought it might be a side-effect of emerging from faster-than-light transport, but he could see no pattern. The doctors prescribed painkillers and stimulants, sometimes in massive doses, in order to keep the crew functional enough to follow Commander Vinton's often capricious orders.

Once the *Conquistador* arrived and established a strong foothold, their orders were to dismantle the ship, retool the engines, and use the remaining fuel to send a bare-bones probe back to Earth. That was how they would deliver a full report to the President as soon as possible. Once Jurudu knew of their success, he could build a second wave of faster-than-light ships for the next phase of colonization.

Now that he had more accurate observations, the Commander could develop realistic settlement scenarios. After a week, he called Andre into his office for another preparatory briefing. Sendy Montoir was already there for the meeting.

The First Officer had brought something with her, which she presented. "Commander, I know you are anxious to plant our flag on the new planet. I'd like to propose a revised banner that bears the colors of old Earth and the seal of President Jurudu, but also shows the star Tau Ceti and a green leaf to symbolize our new beginning." She unfurled the prototype she had created.

Vinton's face turned sour. "We already have a flag to erect."

"True, but it's the banner from *old* Earth, and we'll be on a new world. Our flag should reflect that."

The Commander stood from his desk. "We aren't even three months gone from Earth, and you're already speaking treason against President Jurudu?"

Montoir blinked at him. "Treason, sir? We are separate from Earth. We may be loyal to the principles of the President, but he can no longer be our leader. There's a twelve-year transmission delay to Earth. It would take a quarter-century for us to send a single question and get an answer. When we convert the *Conquistador*'s engines and send the ship's shell back home with our report, that'll be our last direct interaction unless and until Earth builds more FTL ships. And that could take decades, if they do it at all!"

Although Andre agreed with Montoir, he was reluctant to show support for her idea; he knew Vinton all too well. He said, "First Officer, the Commander was placed in charge of this operation because of his lifelong demonstrated ability to follow the President's orders without question...no matter what those orders might be. He is doing the same thing now."

Vinton gave him an odd look, as if wondering what he meant, but Montoir remained insistent. "We have to be realistic, Commander. We need to form our own government."

"*I* am the government!" Vinton snatched the banner and tore it in half along one of the seams.

21

THE *BEACON* RECEIVED ANOTHER MESSAGE from Earth four years after Jurudu's announcement of the FTL discovery. This transmission was equally troubling, and substantially changed Jorie's understanding of how far along Earth's other colony project had come.

She reviewed the new transmission in the Captain's cabin—*her* cabin now. Unfortunately, Captain Andropolis had not lived long enough to receive the new report. She had passed away quietly in her sleep only two days earlier. The funeral plans were in process, and Jorie continued the primary business of the ship.

Even though Jorie had been appointed to the role upon Andropolis's retirement, she had never moved into the official

Captain's quarters. Carrick, Burton, and Carrie would move into the new rooms soon enough, but not yet. The old woman's death was still too raw. For now, Jorie just wanted to be alone in a place where she could remember her mentor.

Kora Andropolis had been her closest friend, someone who had recognized and fostered Jorie's potential from the time she was fourteen. Jorie loved her own parents very much, but Andropolis had made her what she was. The Captain had guided the slowship for nineteen years, longer than some Captains, less than others...but it wasn't a contest.

Long ago, Jorie had vowed to be the slowship's best Captain ever. She had expected to face tremendous leadership challenges when the giant vessel arrived at Sarbras; she also looked forward to the joy of planting seeds and establishing a foothold on a virgin world. But she had never expected the specter of war with the world they had left behind.

The new message from Earth was brief, sent by a scientist-administrator named Andre Pellar. On the image, he looked hurried, as if he wasn't authorized to send the transmission. He revealed that he was the man who had appended the FTL probe data so the *Beacon* planetary scientists could get a better view of their new planet.

"There has been a great setback to our project," said Andre Pellar. "Unrest on Earth. Many protest the crushing expense of building the *Conquistador*, and others do not believe we should seize Sarbras just when the *Beacon* is about to arrive. Some are simply discontented with President Jurudu."

He paused, swallowed visibly. "A terrible accident occurred at Complex Alpha during the testing of the FTL engines. It was sabotaged. Our chief scientist was killed, and I was ordered to start again from scratch. There will be a delay, but I cannot say how long. At least several years. But President Jurudu is intent on reaching Sarbras first and establishing a firm presence there. I...I thought it important to inform you. So you can be prepared when you finally reach Tau Ceti."

Then, as if he feared being caught, Pellar ended the transmission.

Jorie sat back in silence, astonished by the news, wishing she could share her thoughts with Captain Andropolis. She replayed the transmission, listening for nuances, and paced around the cabin, pondering. It seemed the *Beacon* had been given a reprieve; with such a huge setback, maybe the whole FTL project had fallen apart in the intervening years. Or maybe their rushed ship had already launched and established a colony—more likely, a military base—on Sarbras.

Either way, the message gave Jorie a glimpse into how dark and violent Earth's civilization had become. Having lived all her life on the *Beacon*, she didn't want anything to do with those people.

Four years earlier, the *Beacon* had accelerated, burning the fuel reserves to push them forward while saving enough to apply more than a month of hard deceleration at the end of their journey. According to calculations, they would shave another half a year off of their trip.

In the meantime, preparing for the worst case, Jorie assigned teams of *Beacon* engineers to develop potential weapons, basic and traditional systems as well as some imaginative designs. No one had any idea what sort of offensive capabilities the Earth ship might possess, but at least the slowship would not be completely defenseless when they reached Tau Ceti. And arriving nine months early would add to the element of surprise.

Resigned, Jorie released Andre Pellar's transmission so that everyone aboard the slowship could hear it and draw their own conclusions. Knowledge was their best defense. None of the Captains before her had censored reports, and Jorie would not start now.

She'd worry about the repercussions among the crewmember-colonists later. Right now, she had a funeral to worry about.

✦

Images of Captain Burton Pellar's memorial service remained vivid in her mind, though she had been only fourteen at the time. Nevertheless, Jorie reviewed the ship's records of the funeral for help in deciding what to say and how to say it. She feared that she would begin to weep when she said the words that celebrated the Captain's life. As the leader of the *Beacon* now, it wouldn't do for Jorie to burst into tears like a little girl.

Jorie drew strength from an old journal entry in which her mentor confessed that she was afraid she might burst into tears while delivering Captain Pellar's eulogy. Jorie smiled. She would never have guessed it. Captain Andropolis had been a pillar of strength, a true leader.

Jorie would have to do the same. After all, Kora had believed in Jorie.

Somehow, she got through it. The listeners mourned; some of them sniffled and cried, while others remained stoic. They needed stability now more than ever; uncertainty about the threat from Earth's new colonists frightened them, and the prospect of finally arriving at Sarbras made them tense. Fortunately, they also had confidence in Captain Jorie Platt.

But she would need more than confidence to lead them. And they would have no answers until they actually approached the planet.

According to her instructions, Andropolis's body was wrapped up, given full honors, and sent gently away into the universe. The *Beacon* was so close to its destination now, in the midst of heavy deceleration, that the old Captain would drift on the fringes of the Tau Ceti system. A poignant end, Jorie thought.

Jorie felt drained. Two hours after the funeral, she was sitting alone in the Captain's private room off the bridge, letting Carrick take the children so she could contemplate and grieve, when she received an emergency summons: a large disturbance had set off alarms on Deck 17.

Jorie rushed to Nigel Rosenburg's office and showroom, where a group of frightened colonists had gathered in the hall, begging the city planner to stop. His assistant was crying.

Rosenburg had devoted most of his life to designing theoretical colony utopias for Sarbras. Now, with reddened eyes, disheveled hair, and despairing groans, he smashed his most recent model, an airy city with tall diamond towers and looping arches. Using a cudgel, he battered it into shrapnel.

Jorie pushed her way into his office. "Mr. Rosenburg!"

Looking at her, he said, "What's the point? This is all wasted. Those people from Earth will seize everything. You heard the message—they are barbarians! They'll enslave us and destroy whatever we want to build. This is all wasted—*wasted*. And the Captain is dead!"

He lifted his club again and smashed the transparent wall that held his domed undersea city submerged in an aquarium. The transparent pane shattered, and water gushed onto the floor.

"The Captain is very much alive, Mr. Rosenburg," Jorie said. "*I* am the Captain."

Rosenburg said, "And who knows what we'll find on Sarbras?"

"*Exactly*. Who knows? We have to hope. Maybe our cousins from Earth won't want to harm us...or maybe they never launched their ship at all."

He shook his head; his shirt was drenched from the broken aquarium. "They're violent. Saboteurs blew up a facility, killed people—and those were the people on *our* side! What sort of place has Earth become? Who solves problems like that? They are not like us. We invested centuries to achieve this dream and escape that sort of nightmare. We earned our new planet—but now they think they can just take it?"

Jorie put her arm around him. "No, they can't, Mr. Rosenburg. As I told you, I am the Captain. And I mean to do something about it. This whole voyage, from the time the *Beacon* left Earth, has been a leap of faith. Please, keep your faith in me for a little while longer."

22

As the *Conquistador* approached the planet, Commander Vinton grew more impatient and agitated, partially because of the migraines and FTL illness that some of the crew suffered. During the final weeks of travel, he imposed tighter restrictions, made shipwide announcements ranting against the selfish *Beacon* colonists for all the damage they had done on Earth by stealing so many prime resources. It was old news, but the Commander seemed obsessed with reminding them. Repeatedly.

Tapping into Vinton's edgy mood, Andre asked his permission to disseminate President Jurudu's original speech that announced the goals of the *Conquistador* Project. "It would be good for them to hear again why we're here," he said. And the Commander agreed.

Andre also included unedited archival reports of the *Beacon's* departure from Earth more than two centuries earlier. The news footage would show the *Conquistador* crew how the human race had viewed the grand gamble at the time. The current crewmembers had heard only propaganda-filtered reports, but thanks to the full historical library Andre had brought aboard the FTL ship, he could show the original files that had not been broadcast in more than a century.

Commander Vinton treated that part of his request with some skepticism. "Why include the original broadcasts? I don't see how they are important." He squeezed his eyes shut and rubbed his temples.

"To understand our enemy, Commander. If we are going to encounter the *Beacon's* descendants, shouldn't our entire crew know as much about them as possible?"

"I see your point. Permission granted." He looked ill, and anxious just to send him away.

Andre doubted the Commander would watch the original broadcasts, considering them a waste of time.

First Officer Montoir encouraged everyone aboard to view the complete file. The broadcasts portrayed the *Beacon* in a much different light from President Jurudu's slanted summaries. And, thanks to Andre's careful selection of crewmembers, many aboard the *Conquistador* would recognize the names of ancestors and distant relatives. Maybe they would begin to ponder....

The Commander instituted regular drills and war games. As the ship closed in on Sarbras, their telescopes mapped mountain ranges, waterways, and forested lands in great detail; Vinton marked the most desirable territory, already staking his claims on the map.

Looking at the charts in the bridge office, Sendy Montoir furrowed her brow. She had become more outspoken against Vinton's overtly aggressive plans since their arrival in the Tau Ceti system. "How are we going to claim and hold so much of the landscape with only a thousand colonists, Commander?"

He was more short-tempered than usual, from the stimulants the doctors had given him to counteract lingering space sickness. "We'll do it because it's necessary! We should have a year or more to prepare before the *Beacon* arrives. If we can intercept and neutralize that ship, we have nothing to worry about."

Abruptly dismissing her and Andre, Vinton called on the crew to engage in another set of war games.

✦

The following day, Commander Vinton summoned Andre to his private cabin. From his image on the screen, he looked furious. "I need you here without delay, Dr. Pellar. These are grave matters." Vinton terminated the transmission before Andre could ask questions.

Andre swallowed hard, feeling cold inside, but he had no doubts, no reservations. He had already made preparations. Maybe this would finally be the time. Commander Karl Vinton had set his life's course long ago and made his choices. The consequences followed of their own accord.

When he entered the Commander's quarters, Vinton stood there agitated, his face flushed, his red hair unruly. Inside the chamber, Andre spotted First Officer Montoir secured to the chair, her wrists cuffed, her expression a combination of indignation and fear.

Vinton puffed up his chest. "Dr. Pellar, I called you here as my formal witness, as senior civilian representative aboard the *Conquistador*. I am about to issue a summary judgment against my First Officer. Due to the gravity of the situation, I wish to follow the forms precisely."

Andre glanced at Montoir, noted the Commander's frenetic movements and the flush on his face. Vinton's eyes were bloodshot.

"What summary judgment?"

The First Officer's eyes flashed, and she yanked at the metal cuffs that secured her to the chair arms. "He is sick. His authority is slipping through his fingers, and we haven't even reached the planet yet." She sounded like an annoyed parent at the edge of her patience.

He has been sick for a long time, Andre thought, but did not voice his words.

Vinton pounced on her outburst. "There! Another example of how she tries to undermine my command. We cannot allow insubordination at this most crucial time. We must quash any potential mutiny."

"Mutiny?" Andre could see the shine of paranoia in Vinton's eyes. "You'll need evidence of that, sir."

The Commander reached into a drawer of his small desk unit and withdrew the torn remnants of the alternative flag that Montoir had created. "The evidence is all around us. You were present when the First Officer suggested we replace the flag of President Jurudu, that we create our own government and ignore the command structure from Earth."

"I believe that was just a suggestion." Andre remained calm, his voice as hard as stone. "And a reasonable one, sir, considering that we are effectively cut off from all communication with Earth."

"I thought you were more loyal to me, Dr. Pellar," the Commander growled. "Very well, I have plenty of concrete evidence. Recall that I spent years working for the Surveillance & Security Bureau."

A chill went down Andre's back. His hands clenched into fists. "Yes, sir. I know that full well."

Pressing a control on his desk, Vinton played a fuzzy audio recording of a voice that sounded like Sendy Montoir, filtered out of a noisy background. She said, "How is the Commander going to manage a thousand colonists? When we're building a new *home*, we can't just impose the same political structure and austerity measures as we faced on Earth. Old thinking patterns. He doesn't have his head on straight!"

Vinton looked indignant, as if her guilt were self-evident. Bound to the chair, Montoir paled, not from guilt at what she had said, but because the Commander had recorded her at all.

Andre said, "That's just conversation, sir. Are you monitoring all of our conversations?"

With a sniff, Vinton played another surreptitious recording of First Officer Montoir, this one from an exercise chamber. "He was given command of the expedition to Tau Ceti, but everything changes once we arrive," she said. "Sarbras will be our world. I'm going to propose that we hold elections. As a group, we should all have a part in deciding what kind of colony we want to be. If a majority chooses to elect Karl Vinton as their first leader, then that's fine. But they must have that choice."

Montoir said from her chair, "I don't deny any of it. It's rational discourse. Do you truly think everyone aboard wants our new colony world to turn into a military camp?"

"Yes, if necessary!" Vinton snapped. To silence her, he shoved a piece of cloth into her mouth. His hands shook, as if with palsy. "Enough of this charade. The *Conquistador* can't afford the disruption of an open trial when we are so close to arriving at the planet." His gaze skated over to land on Andre. "I called you here, Dr. Pellar, so that you could hear the evidence and witness my command decision."

Stepping behind his desk, Vinton opened a drawer and withdrew a long hypodermic needle filled with an orange liquid. He held it up. "I learned this from President Jurudu. After the disaster at Complex Alpha, it became obvious that the explosion was not an accident, but the work of a terrorist group. I worked closely on those investigations myself." He came around the desk to stand over the First Officer. "However, so as to maintain calm among the populace, President Jurudu chose not to expose those terrorists and create a panic. Instead, he simply took care of the seditious group, maintained the fiction of a tragic accident, and let the suspicions die."

He sniffed. "That's the best solution here. Rather than point out my First Officer's treason, I will carry out the execution here. The official report will state that she died from an unfortunate heart attack."

The First Officer glared at Vinton and thrashed, trying to yank her hands free of the metal cuffs.

"Criminals must be punished, Commander," Andre said, surprising himself by sounding cool and logical. "That is a fundamental tenet of our civilization. President Jurudu stated it himself many times."

"Indeed." Vinton appeared relieved that Andre did not challenge him. "Criminals must be punished."

Andre stepped closer to the Commander, who raised the syringe of poison. "But there's one more thing I'd like to bring to your attention, if I may, sir?"

Vinton glanced at him, distracted. "What is it?"

Andre slipped his sleeve aside and fired the paralytic dart he had carried for days. The tiny needle buried itself in the Commander's neck.

Vinton squawked, cried out, and then slumped; Andre caught him, eased the man into his desk chair as the poison-filled hypodermic dropped to the deck with a thin clatter. The Commander's shoulders and arms twitched, but otherwise he did not move.

Shackled to her chair, First Officer Montoir stared at him in disbelief as he yanked the gag from her mouth. "What the hell?"

Andre said, "He's paralyzed, but unharmed. The drug will wear off in an hour. In the meantime, I need to show you another case. You can act as *my* witness. Please?" Andre used the key Vinton had left on his desk and released Montoir from her cuffs. "I needed to use a paralytic dart because I knew he wouldn't sit still and let me present the facts."

"You don't have to convince me," she said, standing up and rubbing her wrists.

"Yes," he said. "Yes, I do." He bent down, picked up the deadly syringe from where it had fallen on the deck, and placed it in plain view on the Commander's desk. "A cousin of mine, Burton Pellar, was the ninth Captain of the *Beacon*. A large percentage of the *Conquistador*'s crew also have family connections to the colonists who left Earth long ago." He cast a withering glance at Commander Vinton. "This man, however, does not. He is something else entirely. Let me show you."

The Commander seemed to be struggling, but the paralytic prevented all movement other than a few small twitches of his hands. Andre nudged Vinton's head, aligning his open eyes with the screen. "I want you to watch this, sir, though I don't know how you could have forgotten."

On the desk's display screen, Andre tapped into his own private library and retrieved the files he had sifted out of classified government records. He called up an image of Renee Sinha. Just looking at her, he could feel the knife of regret in his chest.

"Many years ago, this woman was my partner. I didn't love her enough at the time, and I learned that too late." His voice cracked; he drew a breath and continued. "She was a vocal supporter of the *Beacon* and insisted that those colonists should be allowed to achieve their dream. She didn't like the idea of an upstart, faster-than-light ship stealing the dream they had followed for over two hundred years. She tried to convince me to abandon the *Conquistador* Project.

"Some of Renee's friends were more militant. After the explosions at Complex Alpha, security troops came to our apartment and took her away for questioning. I never heard from her again. I knew nothing about what had happened to her. I was told to forget...but I never did." He leaned closer to the frozen commander. "Did *you* forget, Interrogation Officer Vinton?"

He pulled up the dossier and displayed the Surveillance & Security Bureau's summary report, and the weight grew heavier inside him. He felt paralyzed himself, afraid to show the rest, but he knew he had to.

First Officer Montoir watched in fascination, but did not understand.

Andre said, "The Bureau rigorously questioned Renee. The officer in charge of the interrogation was Karl Vinton. He kept her alive for more than two weeks before he killed her. That much information was in the Summary Report."

Once Andre had found the report confirming that Renee was dead, he wished he had not opened the other documents. But after wondering for so long, he had to know. He swallowed hard, and forced himself to go on. He played the detailed recordings, pausing at vital points, and made Vinton watch.

The Interrogation Officer had beaten Renee, demanding to know about her involvement with the terrorists—she had confessed to that soon enough. She'd been part of a larger dissident group, but had not participated in planting the bombs herself, although her connections in the chemical factory had allowed her to supply some materials. She was guilty; Andre did not try to pretend otherwise.

On the night of the explosions, Renee had lured him out of the lab to the coffee club in order to keep him safe. Interrogation Officer Vinton asked how Andre was involved with the dissidents, but she insisted he had no connection. Vinton didn't believe her. He wanted to be sure, so he kept demanding that she expose Andre's involvement. When she refused, he broke all the fingers on her left hand with a sound like snapping dry wicker. She whimpered, but didn't scream.

Renee still refused to implicate him. Then Vinton raped her, relishing the process, knowing that every moment was being recorded. Afterward, he broke all the fingers in her right hand and raped her again. He continued to demand that she expose Andre as part of the dissidents.

"I was naïve," Andre said now in a hollow voice. "I might have been a patsy, but I had nothing to do with the movement. Renee could have lied and implicated me, saved herself some pain, but she didn't. This man, this monster destroyed her."

Tears filled his eyes and his voice was hoarse. Montoir looked sickened and disgusted. Turning back to the desk, Andre blanked the screen and faced the paralyzed Commander, but he spoke to Sendy Montoir. "Is this the type of leader we want on our new world? Is this the seed from Earth that we want to plant?"

The First Officer stepped forward, looming over Vinton. "Criminals need to be punished. The Commander said it himself." She lifted the poison syringe that he had intended to use on her.

"I've hated him ever since I found out," Andre said. "I should be the one to kill him."

"No. Because for you it would be revenge, and this should be *justice*—the start of justice on a new world." Without hesitation or ceremony, the First Officer slid the hypodermic needle into Vinton's neck and depressed the plunger.

The Commander twitched, spasmed, but the paralytic minimized his movements, and he slowly slumped onto his desk. "A tragic and unexpected heart attack," she announced. "That's all the crew needs to know."

Andre felt weak. So long…Now that he knew what had happened to Renee and had finally seen the man punished, he had achieved a more important goal than reaching another star system. He tried to find something profound to say, something appropriate for Renee, but his throat remained dry.

Andre was stunned. "Are you sure it wasn't revenge for you, too? He was going to execute you."

"We can open a full investigation if we need to," Montoir said, and now she started trembling, as if the magnitude of what she'd done had just caught up with her. "I don't want to set up the same kind of society on Sarbras as President Jurudu imposed on Earth."

Suddenly, alarms rang through the ship, calling all personnel to their stations. The intercom in the Commander's quarters activated, and a gruff voice from the bridge spilled out. "It's the *Beacon*, sir! The ship has arrived."

23

As the generation ship entered the Tau Ceti system under heavy deceleration, Jorie issued orders to reduce the *Beacon*'s energy usage as much as possible. They ran silent, inbound to the planet they intended to claim as their home. "Don't want to let them know we're coming. No need to give the *Conquistador* any advantage." She sounded fully like the Captain now.

For months now, everyone aboard the slowship had scrambled to prepare for a possible hostile encounter upon their arrival. They listened for any transmissions, any indications of an established colony or military base on the planet. The *Conquistador* was definitely not trying to keep its presence hidden, and it radiated heat and transmissions like an alarm bell. The FTL ship from Earth had arrived ahead of them, and now it headed across the Tau Ceti system toward its target.

Jorie took heart in learning that the *Conquistador* had not established a base on the planet yet. They weren't entrenched.

Nevertheless, the *Beacon* had to sneak toward their new home like thieves in the night, in hopes of remaining unnoticed until they could assess the situation. This was not the way Jorie had imagined the *Beacon*'s voyage would end at Sarbras. Reaching the finish line after such a marathon, the thousands of colonists should have been able to rejoice, to step forward as pioneers on an untouched landscape.

The generation ship, after two centuries of building up velocity, was going even faster, although braking as it descended toward the planet. It really would be a race.

"New readings, Captain," said her new deputy, a rugged and athletic young man named Juan Antero. "At our speed, we'll intercept them soon."

"Their messages didn't sound friendly," she said, "so let's hope either it was all bluster...or that our new defenses function as predicted."

"We're ready, Captain."

Jorie took her own station on the bridge deck. "Keep an eye on them, Mr. Antero. Let me know the moment they notice us."

For generations, the crewmember-colonists had studied physics, science, and industry, prepared to meet the challenges that the new world offered. Lately, though, the best minds aboard had devoted their skills to developing defensive weapons. After investing generations in this gamble, they would not allow any brash latecomers to take Sarbras from them. Jorie knew her people were a force to be reckoned with.

As the *Beacon* approached Sarbras, high-res telescopes showed the *Conquistador*'s sharp lines and the massive FTL engines that had driven the vessel to Tau Ceti in such a short time. The ominous, aggressive look of the newcomer ship made Jorie's skin crawl.

"Make sure our new gunports are open and visible."

"All eighty of them, Captain?"

"All eighty—no point in holding anything back."

Jorie longed to turn her attention to the beautiful planet that hung before them like a trophy. With its blue skies and puffy clouds, the blurry outlines of continents...it very much resembled the images of Earth they had studied in the slow-ship's libraries for generations. Such a world had filled their dreams, passed from parent to child, again and again and again. Sarbras was supposed to be the light at the end of the tunnel.

Before long, a signal pinged out. "Looks like they spotted us, Captain," Antero said.

A gruff male voice said, "This is the Earth ship *Conquistador*. We claim this planet in the name of President Jurudu. This is Major Wexler. We are in the process of establishing our colony, and we commandeer the equipment and supplies aboard the *Beacon* for the good of all. Make no aggressive moves. We will discuss the terms of your assimilation."

Cries of dismay rippled throughout her bridge crew. "Not a very nice way to say hello," Jorie said. "He's full of himself. Are our defenses operational?"

"Operational, Captain," said Deputy Antero. *But untested.*

Jorie had rehearsed this moment a thousand times in her mind; now she knew it was a worst-case scenario. She sat straight and confident as she activated the channel to address the other ship. "This is Captain Jorie Platt of the *Beacon*. Our forbears staked their claim on this world more than two hundred years ago when we left Earth. This is our home, but there's plenty of room. No need to get greedy—neither of us needs a whole planet."

"We will take and hold Sarbras by any means necessary, and you have no choice but to cooperate. We have orders from the President on Earth."

Jorie felt cold and calm. "Oh really? Let me speak with him."

That unsettled the brash man. "Not possible."

"My point exactly."

Flustered, Major Wexler said, "Commander Vinton is on his way. You would be wise to deal with me instead. Surrender and allow yourself to be boarded and inventoried."

"We will not. Our people are independent, and we intend to build our own colony."

Wexler seemed very anxious, as if eager to resolve the situation before his Commander arrived. He didn't care that Jorie heard him bellow orders. "Fire the first missile battery—target their engines only. They won't be needing them anymore." He turned his cold blue eyes back to Jorie. "This is just a warning shot, Captain Platt."

Like deadly wasps, five missiles leaped out of gunports on the side of the *Conquistador*, streaking across the distance between the ships, lit by hot-burning exhaust plumes. The Major's targeting was excellent.

"Brace yourselves, everyone!" Jorie shouted. Just in case.

But when the missiles came close to the hull, they slowed and shimmered, striking a barrier like energy gelatin, caught in the barrier field like a fly in honey. The warheads exploded, but the energy was directed out into space, away from the giant ship.

She heaved a slight sigh, but tried not to show Wexler her relief. Her scientists had had years to plan, all the time in the world to develop their own ideas, to test them, to apply them to keep the *Beacon* safe.

Wexler looked astonished on the screen.

"We are fully prepared to defend our rights, Major." Now that the FTL ship had fired on them and demonstrated their true intentions, she had to shock them, establish the *Beacon*'s position of strength. Jorie turned to her deputy. "Mr. Antero, fire gunport number two. Note that it is not my intention to inflict immediate damage on the *Conquistador*, but make sure the plasma charge detonates close enough for them to feel it."

"Yes, Captain."

Jorie met Major Wexler's suddenly fearful expression on the screen. "This is *our* warning shot."

Antero gave the order, and gunport number two spewed out a crackling blue plasma ball that surrounded a fusion warhead of metallic tritium. It tumbled across space and detonated near the bow of the FTL ship. Jorie winced as a double shockwave sent out concentric spheres of energy brighter than Tau Ceti's sun.

The weapon was a new design that her engineers had developed using interstellar hydrogen gathered by their ramscoop. It had been tested once in deep space, and Jorie knew what to expect. The explosion was spectacular, and it should have knocked out half of the sensors aboard the FTL ship without causing permanent damage. She hoped.

✦

Leaving Commander Vinton's cabin, they closed and secured the door. Andre and Montoir looked at each other, sickened.

Alarms sounded throughout all decks, and Major Wexler's increasingly strident demands filled the shipwide intercom. "Commander Vinton, please respond!"

"I need to go to the bridge," the First Officer said. "I will assume command and open communications with the *Beacon*."

Andre felt dizzy. Yes, that was what Renee would have wanted….

They reached the bridge just as the *Beacon*'s completely unexpected weapon whirled in front of the *Conquistador*'s bow and detonated, sending thunderous echoes through the decks. Many bridge stations erupted in sparks from the sudden surge, and most of the sensor screens went blind.

"What the hell was that?" Andre shouted.

"They've opened fire on us!" said Major Wexler.

Montoir went straight to the command chair. When he saw the First Officer, Wexler's flicker of relief changed to confusion. "Where is the Commander?"

Her announcement sounded breathless, but offhand. "Commander Vinton has been the victim of…an unfortunate heart attack." She faced the bridge personnel. "I am now in command."

He reeled. "This is an emergency situation. We need—"

"I said, I am in command!" Montoir snapped. "Report, Major Wexler."

"Yes, uh, Commander. I have already demanded their surrender and fired a warning shot—"

Montoir cut him off. "You have no such authority."

"It was the protocol Commander Vinton laid out for our first encounter. President Jurudu said we could easily take down a group of weak colonists!"

Andre remained astonished. "But the *Beacon*'s not a warship."

As techs scrambled to restore emergency power to the bridge controls, Montoir said, "Perhaps you should have been more prudent, Major. That weapon could have vaporized us." She turned to the comm officer. "Let me talk to them. Maybe I can straighten out this mess."

She positioned herself in the command chair, spoke to the screen that flickered back to life, though the image remained blurred by static. "*Beacon*, please hold your fire. This is First Officer Sendy Montoir of the *Conquistador*. Our Commander is deceased, and the new leadership structure has a somewhat different philosophy about our future here on Sarbras. Please forgive my subordinate Major Wexler, who may have spoken prematurely."

On the one functional screen, Andre watched the *Beacon* grow closer, filling the entire field of view…and then it grew larger still, and even larger. He knew that few people aboard the *Conquistador* truly comprehended the scale of the vast generation ship. There was a reason this vessel had caused such a tremendous drain on Earth's economy: more than a kilometer long, filled with thousands of people, an entire self-contained ecosystem. The *Conquistador* was large, but at more than ten times their size the *Beacon* utterly dwarfed them.

The slowship continued to close the distance, showing rows and rows of active gunports, all of them directed toward the *Conquistador*.

Andre pointed out, "Those weren't there during the ship's construction."

"Eighty gunports in all, Commander," said one of the tactical officers.

"Our weapons did nothing to them," Wexler said. "Five missiles were deflected, didn't leave a scratch."

"You fired *five missiles* at them?" Montoir cried. "Major Wexler, you are relieved of duty until further notice."

"Commander! This is a crisis—"

"A crisis you provoked. If you don't confine yourself to quarters immediately, I'll find a sidearm and shoot you myself."

Andre knew she would do it.

As Wexler left the bridge, reeling, Andre had an idea. The thousand crewmembers knew him as the project head hand-picked by President Jurudu, as well as the close confidante of Commander Vinton. He had selected most of the crew, based on his own criteria. Even Major Wexler likely didn't know he was a distant relative of one of the *Beacon*'s former Captains.

"Could I address the ships, Commander? Both the *Conquistador* and the *Beacon*?"

Montoir looked at him and nodded. "After what we've been through, Dr. Pellar, I'll give you the benefit of the doubt."

Andre spoke on the shipwide intercom, knowing his words were also being transmitted to the looming genera-tion ship. "This is Andre Pellar. I built this ship and guided this project from its inception. I chose most of the crew. Of the thousand crewmembers who intend to settle here on Sar-bras, *eight hundred* are related to the original colonists who departed two hundred years ago. Most of the people aboard the *Beacon* and the *Conquistador* are distant cousins."

He let that sink in, before speaking primarily to those on his own ship. "President Jurudu is not here, and we are not going back to Earth. Look at the planet below: that is our new home." Then he indicated the screen where the *Bea-con* hung as large as a moon. "And look at that ship—it's full of people who have been preparing for generations to make a home on an unknown world. They have equipment, seed stock, embryos, and knowledge—probably more than we do.

"They are not weaklings or cowards! Imagine what it took for more than three thousand people to survive—and appar-ently thrive—sealed in a ship for more than two centuries. They don't have to be our rivals! Together, we could build a much stronger colony."

The *Beacon*'s Captain finally responded. "Sounds like you may have a few reasonable people aboard after all. So, Dr. Pellar, it's no coincidence that your last name is the same as one of our Captains'?"

"None at all, Captain Platt. I followed each of the reports your ship transmitted to Earth."

Her face looked skeptical, bathed in static on the screen. "We'll hold our fire…until we can be certain of your intentions."

✦

Jorie was surprised, and somewhat pleased, to see the scientist who had appended the probe images of Sarbras and informed them of the terrorist attack on the FTL project.

"Prepare gunport number three," Jorie said in a whisper. "Just in case."

The screen activated again with a transmission from the *Conquistador*, Andre Pellar standing next to Commander Montoir.

Pellar spoke again. "When I built this ship, my vision for it was not the same as the mission President Jurudu gave us. Now that we're here, many things have changed. We are together above an unspoiled planet. You have many resources that will be valuable for establishing a settlement, but we can pull our own weight."

"Captain Platt, I would be willing to shuttle over and meet with you face to face, so that we can make plans," Commander Montoir said.

"We will hold our weapons in reserve, pending a formal agreement," Jorie said. "But come aboard. Let's build a world together."

She switched off the transmission before anyone aboard the *Conquistador* could see her immense relief.

Of the eighty gunports that studded the hull of the *Beacon*, only two of them functioned anyway. The rest were just window dressing.

24

THE TWO COLONY SHIPS RODE side-by-side above the planet that would be their new home. A network of observation and mapping satellites had been dispatched to scout for mineral deposits. The air was breathable, the temperature mild…a whole wide-open world.

As the first shuttles prepared to depart, Jorie went down to the *Beacon*'s large launching bay, ready to take her flight down to humanity's new home. Commander Montoir would also join her, and they had agreed to dispense with any nonsense of who got to take the first step. They would do it together.

Montoir and Andre Pellar both came over to the *Beacon* to meet the generation ship's Captain and colonists. Jorie could tell that they seemed even more awed by the enormous slowship than they were by the planet itself.

She and the *Conquistador*'s Commander would fly down together with a small security crew and a few token scientists and high-ranking personnel, evenly divided from the two vessels. The teams would verify that the atmosphere was breathable, that the landing site was stable, but both Jorie and Montoir knew that this was just a political mission, a dramatic event for every person on both ships to witness.

Leaving the first footprints.

"President Jurudu said that only one person in all of human history can ever be *first*," Andre Pellar said. "I won't be going along. Not this time."

Jorie was surprised, but Commander Montoir seemed completely taken aback. "You certainly deserve it. This project owes more to you than to anyone else alive."

"But it doesn't mean anything to me," he said. "And I have other unfinished business."

Jorie said, "For a man who builds faster-than-light engines, you don't seem to be in any hurry."

He shrugged. "The planet will still be there."

Indeed, after the first landing on Sarbras, a rush of survey ships would bring swarms of scientists to study all aspects of the new planet. He would have his chance.

Jorie and Commander Montoir climbed aboard the first shuttle, which was piloted by one of the *Conquistador* soldiers, per Jorie's request, with a *Beacon* copilot. Her own people had practiced in simulators to hone their skills, but the pilots from Earth had practical experience.

As the shuttle rose up on its long-dormant engines and eased toward the bay door, the pilot double-checked the old systems, familiarizing himself with what must have seemed like an antique to him. Jorie looked out at the starry field as the shuttle flew out, pulling away from the giant generation ship and heading toward the tantalizing planet below, like a bird leaving the nest.

As the pilot steadied the flight, an automated system switched on in the cockpit, and the shuttle's comm systems glowed. Jorie noticed and said, "What's that?"

The baffled pilot tried ineffectually to shut down the automated routine.

"It's a pre-recorded message, Captain," said the copilot. He bent over the screen. "Stored for timed delivery, triggered by the launch of the shuttle."

"It's also being broadcast on the open channels," said the pilot. "To the *Beacon* and the *Conquistador.*"

The image of an old woman appeared on the cockpit comm screen, which would also be received by the two large ships. "I am Captain Kora Andropolis. By the time you hear this, I will no longer be alive." Indeed, her face was gaunt, her hair gone, her eyes sunken. "I lived my entire life aboard this ship, and I did my best to guide the *Beacon* to our destination. My predecessor lived his entire life with no hope of reaching Tau Ceti. As did the generations before him.

"But now the *Beacon* has hope. When this message is broadcast, we will be at Sarbras. Others from Earth might be here waiting for us. I hope you have found a way to live together."

She lifted her chin, spoke in a louder voice. "If there are people who have raced here from Earth, please listen. These colonists aboard the *Beacon* are good people who have devoted their lives to creating a new world. Over a journey of nearly twelve light years, we have learned how to live together. Maybe we've learned things that will benefit you as well?"

Listening to Andropolis, tears sprang to Jorie's eyes. The old Captain had recorded this message on her deathbed, finding a way to participate in the arrival at Sarbras, even after her body had been consigned to the stars. Andropolis continued in a scratchy voice. "I'll never see that new home, but I hope the rest of you will. As for surviving together, you'll have to figure that out for yourselves."

With a trembling hand, the old woman reached forward and switched off the recording. Her image vanished into static, and Jorie struggled to maintain her composure.

Commander Montoir looked over at Jorie. "The previous Captain? She speaks good words. I think we can find a way to survive together."

✦

Several days later, Andre returned to the giant generation ship for another meeting with Captain Platt, while the first expeditions dropped down to the surface. Everyone was anxious to set foot on solid ground. They had planning and scouting to do, but now that they had arrived, the crewmember-colonists had all the time in the world.

Over the course of a week, vanguard teams established temporary settlements using prefab building modules; these camps would eventually become colony towns. Biological teams tested the local vegetation to determine if Sarbras biochemistry was compatible with Terran life.

"After the difficulties the human race has faced, we were due for a bit of good luck," Andre said to the Captain.

Looking through the observation windows of the *Beacon*'s bridge, he watched shuttle after shuttle drop down to the surface, carrying the first waves of pioneers and explorers—from both ships. Those people would lay the groundwork and establish settlements and agriculture, while scouts explored the alien landscape. The rest of the colonists would remain aboard the *Beacon* until Sarbras was ready for them. The generation ship could support everyone.

Standing beside him, Jorie nodded. "Now that you've told me more about President Jurudu's regime, I'm more concerned about a response from Earth. Jurudu knows how to build a faster-than-light ship. Once he hears that the *Conquistador* arrived safely, it's only a matter of time before someone else comes." She pressed her lips together. "Instead of focusing entirely on our new colony, we'll have to devote time, energy, and resources to building our defenses and prepare for whatever may come. Do you think he'll remain in power? And that the citizens will put up with the continued expense?"

Andre pondered in silence, then said with a faint smile, "Not if we convince them this mission is a disaster."

Nearby, the *Conquistador* was being dismantled, in accordance with the mission plan. Portions of the ship had been detached and sent down to the surface as ready-made fortresses, or self-contained colony villages. Once the extra structures were disassembled, the FTL drives were intended to carry a messenger probe back home with all available information about the new planet.

Andre continued, "President Jurudu insisted that we send him a full report as soon as possible so he could prepare for the next wave of colonization…but I don't feel obligated to send an *accurate* report. And I believe I have an appropriate message to include with the probe."

He explained his idea, and she chuckled. "There's no rush, Dr. Pellar. Take your time and do it right. We'll only have one chance."

✦

Jorie boarded a shuttle to the surface, taking her husband and two children along. Sendy Montoir was already in charge of the first large settlement on a grassy plain, and the *Conquistador* colonists also went down.

But Andre returned to the FTL ship he had built. He had decided not to set foot on their new planet until he completed his project and could move on with his life.

The *Conquistador*'s bridge deck was vacant. Many of the systems had been burned out by the shockwave from the plasma-fusion blast. The officers' stations looked scarred and empty, the leftovers of a battle zone—exactly what he needed. He even brought Commander Vinton's body back to the bridge and propped it in the command chair; the slack corpse could be used to good effect. To make himself look harried and haggard, Andre had only to remember Renee in those last few images of her monstrous interrogation.

He activated the recording and began abruptly. "President Jurudu, the *Conquistador*'s mission has failed! Commander Vinton is dead. The FTL engines…" He shook his head and gazed at the screen with a tortured expression. "The FTL engines are fatally flawed!

"We did reach Tau Ceti, but the aftereffects on the human mind from faster-than-light transport were…horrific. Seventy-five percent of our crew died outright! The rest suffered from madness—they murdered hundreds more. I've jettisoned the fortress modules and barricaded myself here on the bridge. But I think I can still rig the engines and launch this message back to Earth. I had to warn you!"

He uploaded a flood of images, close-ups of the furious lava field taken from survey satellites over part of one continent—billowing smoke, toxic fumes, spraying magma. Other images showed the mammoth hurricane in the oceans with storm winds higher than any recorded on Earth in centuries.

"And for what?" Andre cried, his voice cracking. "This place is a hellhole! I can't imagine a worse planet to colonize." He began to sob. "Don't use the FTL drive again—it's not worth the risk. The whole mission is a failure, Mr. President, a complete disaster."

He ended the transmission, reviewed it, and decided it was satisfactory.

✦

Over the next week, the rest of the *Conquistador* was disassembled, every useful item removed and ferried either to the planet's surface or over to the *Beacon*. The FTL engines, with their remaining fuel and the probe attachment, carried Andre's distraught but fictional message away from Sarbras.

Jorie stood next to him and watched as the *Conquistador* probe gained distance. Andre turned to her. "Do you think it will work? Was I convincing enough?"

She shrugged. "You convinced me." They both caught their breath as the FTL drive flared and the probe vanished into the gulf of space. Jorie turned to face the wispy clouds, the green continents, the blue oceans of Sarbras. "Right now, we have a whole planet to worry about. First things first."

♈

Introducing
Steven Savile
Kevin J. Anderson

I'VE BEEN A JUDGE in the Writers of the Future Contest since 1996. A couple of times each year, I receive a stack of anonymous manuscripts from the contest administrator, which I'll read; after making my selections, I'm supposed to discard the stories.

When I have tight deadlines and need to get a lot of writing and editing done with very few distractions, I often head to an isolated cabin in the mountains. In late fall of 2002, I took my laptop and the draft chapters in my novel with Brian Herbert, *Dune: The Machine Crusade*, to a rental condo, along with the stack of 3rd Quarter finalist manuscripts for Writers of the Future.

The weather turned cold, and an unexpected snowstorm dumped about a foot of snow, but I'd brought plenty of canned soup, and the rental condo had a nice fireplace. I built a cozy fire, edited Dune chapters, then in between I read the Contest stories. Since I was supposed to discard the manuscripts anyway, I added them to the firewood and brightened the blaze.

One of the stories I liked was called "Bury My Heart at the Garrick."

The following August, during the Writers of the Future workshop in Hollywood, CA, one of the newbie winners introduced himself to me. I didn't know him, since judges don't see the entrants' names on the stories, but he said, "My story was about Houdini trying to escape from Hell." That rang a bell. I answered, "I remember your story. I fed it page by page into the fire as I read it!"

I don't think that was exactly what Steve wanted to hear. In retrospect, maybe my phrasing could have been different....

I didn't know at the time that, even though he had won the Contest as a "new" writer, Steve had already sold a professional story (which never saw print because the magazine went bankrupt), sold a novel (which was returned when the publisher nearly went out of business), gotten and lost a big-name agent, written and sold a pre-teen romance (which was never published because the line was dropped), and sold a four-part TV drama (which was cancelled when MTV bought the network and axed all original programming).

So even before I met him, Steve Savile already had a major impact in the publishing world, mostly disastrous.

But things were looking up. After the Writers of the Future win, he began selling and publishing new work (without destroying the publishers who were kind enough to accept the stories). He got a gig writing the *Vampire Wars* trilogy for Games Workshop, then two Slaine novels for Black Flame, then Dr. Who stories, Torchwood, and Primeval tie-in *Shadow of the Jaguar* (which hit #1 on UK bestseller lists). His original thriller *Silver* was published in hardcover in the US and hit #2 on the UK eBook bestseller lists.

We've kept in touch over the past nine years, and he was my immediate choice as the person to write the second half of the story in *Tau Ceti*. I just received his manuscript, and I've printed it out. I eagerly look forward to reading it.

It's October in the Colorado mountains, and the temperature has dropped. A foot of snow fell last night.

And I've got a fire...

TAU CETI

Book Two
GRASSHOPPER
AND ANTS

STEVEN SAVILE

1

217 years since the Beacon's *departure from Earth.*
Year Zero: Tau Ceti.

FOR ALL OF NIGEL ROSENBURG'S grand designs and the fabulous cities of his imagination, with their towering sky-scrapers and fairy tale diamond towers, the practicalities of setting up a colony on Sarbras meant that their first course of action was to turn the slowship into a temporary land base to build from. It made sense. It was journey's end. The *Beacon* wouldn't be flying on and it had its own fully functioning eco-system and had been their home for their whole lives. Outside was a frightening place. They'd never seen the sky. They'd never had space, which considering they'd only ever had *space*, made Jorie smile. They'd had empty black skies, but nothing like this. She stood on the ramp looking out at the lush pas-tures spread out before her, and in the distance, snow-capped mountains. Sarbras was alive.

Unsurprisingly, perhaps, some of their number were trau-matized by the sheer *freedom* Sarbras offered. So much so it turned them almost agoraphobic and left them afraid to set foot outside. It would come, given time, Jorie knew. Change was always hard to cope with, and such a radical change was always going to take some getting used to.

They looked to her for an example.

Jorie had adapted well to the role of the *Beacon*'s eleventh and final Captain; a post that had been thrust upon her by her mentor's untimely death. She looked up now at the bright blue sky, wondering if Kora Andropolis was looking down on them. She hoped she was. Jorie had yet to set foot planet-side. Her children, Burton and Carrie, had already been out, playing in the dirt with Carrick. She couldn't have stopped him if she wanted to, but one of the things she loved most about her husband was that he could still get so excited about mud. As Captain, though, there was something symbolic about setting foot on Sarbras, so she had made excuses, found tasks that urgently needed her attention on-board, and hoped no one noticed she kept avoiding going outside, before now.

Mechanical arms lurched forward, stabbing at the ground as the buckets scraped up earth and stone. There were black scorch marks streaking around the hull where the engines had burned. The buckets dragged up huge scoops of earth as the *Beacon* dug in. It made an infernal racket.

Jorie had dispatched two scouting parties in the days since they sent the first shuttle down, because as much as she trusted technology there was nothing like honest first-hand accounts of terrain from people she trusted. They hadn't reported back yet. The first reports should be back by sundown. There was so much to do before then.

Sendy Montoir and Andre Pellar flanked her on either side.

They exchanged a look that spoke volumes. Circumstance had thrown them together, there was an air of complicity around them, making the pair seem as thick as thieves, and yet she noticed that they never seemed to touch. Not even accidentally, a brush of hand against hand or arm against arm. It was all in glances and words, subtle signals that someone not looking for them could never have seen.

They were well-suited, Jorie thought, contemplating a role of meddlesome matchmaker, and she liked both of them well enough from the little time they'd spent together, grateful that between them they'd managed to avoid christening their new world in blood, but for all that, there was something *wrong*. She could sense something, some kind of damage that held them apart. She had no idea what it was, but they weren't the only ones off *Conquistador* who shared that vibe. Jorie felt stupid for paying attention to her gut, but Kora Andropolis had drilled home the importance of instinct time and time again. A Captain needed to trust her head, her heart and her gut, because if one failed the others almost certainly wouldn't.

There were one thousand men and women who seemed to be just ever so slightly *wrong*. That was the only way she could describe it. There was nothing she could put her finger on. Nothing that marked them as different. They just seemed hungrier for life. They consumed it voraciously. They burned through more energy, were more vibrant and just burned brighter. Perhaps it was the first strands of some sort of divergent evolution going on? They were all born out of the same cultural stock, but it was a stock that had divided two centuries earlier. One strand had been driven by hope for the future, the other by despair over the past. Could it be that simple? Could it just be that they were the same but fundamentally different in how they embraced life?

Could it have been so *bad* back on Earth?

Or was it something else? That thought niggled at the back of Jorie's mind, but she didn't have time to dwell on it. They had enough challenges ahead without imagining new ones. There was a whole new world out there waiting for her, and a lot of expectant eyes on her.

"It's time," Jorie said. She drew in a deep breath. Jorie had dreamed about this moment every single day of her life.

She walked down the metal ramp, looking slowly from left to right, taking it all in. This was it, their new home. It really was beautiful. It was hard to imagine that two hundred years of traveling was over. She gripped the flagpole in her hand tighter, her knuckles blanching white. It was a purely symbolic gesture, but still, it felt strange to plant this new banner.

The others filed down the ramp behind her, some moving to the left, others to the right, to form a horseshoe around Jorie. She stood in the center, clutching the flagpole in both hands. They all looked at her. She felt the weight of their expectation. And in that moment realized she was equal to it. Right up until then she had still doubted it. A little self-doubt was healthy though, or so Jorie believed.

She saw friendly faces in the crowd, Carrick beaming at her, her children looking up at her with impatience because they wanted to be off causing mischief, the Noah who had lived long enough to see the fulfillment of his duties, engineers, cadets, people she had spent her entire life with.

In stark contrast to today, the last ceremony they had all gathered for had been a sober affair. Yes, it was a celebration of Kora Andropolis's life, but saying goodbye was always hard, but so close to journey's end it was heart-breaking. Jorie would have traded five years off her life just to have Kora beside her now to see this, to breathe in perfect air and see a real blue sky, but there was no one out there to take that deal.

She looked up at the sky again.

This was the beginning of an era.

The weight of history was in front of her.

They were breaking ground on their new home. This was a joyous occasion, the end to their wanderings, and yet she felt so heart-heavy.

Carrick Platt smiled that smile at her. She half expected him to throw a handful of mud at her, or at least smear it on his face to make her laugh. Just thinking about it was enough to make her smile for a moment. And sometimes a moment was all it took.

The crews of the *Beacon* and the *Conquistador* took up their places around the arc. Jorie looked from face to face. These were her people. She had never felt so proud of anything in her life. Proud that they had persevered, that they had done so together, and that they stood here united under a bright blue sky. This was the fulfillment of two hundred years of human endeavor. This was a moment to be savored.

No wonder the flagpole felt like it weighed so much.

Jorie looked at the flag.

Sendy Montoir had shown her the design; well, shown her scraps of torn fabric and explained the symbolism behind them, the night before. The final design had changed slightly since then, given conversations the two of them had shared. This was a new beginning. Jorie had taken the initiative to have a proper flag made up from Sendy's design. The flag bore marked similarity to the old flag, with the united colors of old Earth making up most of it, but President Jurudu's seal had been replaced at the heart of it by the star of Tau Ceti.

Seconds away from planting a brand new flag in the virgin soil of Sarbras part of Jorie's mind screamed: *what are you doing? This is treason*, but she refused to listen to it. They owed no loyalty to the old world. Sendy and Andre Pellar had convinced her of that, banishing any last lingering doubts she might have had based on Jurudu's own transmissions. No, they were free now. This wasn't Earth 2, this was Sarbras.

"My friends, both old and new," she called out, her voice stronger, more composed and sure of itself, than she felt. "I did not for a minute think it would fall to me to make this speech, but it is with immense pride and gratitude to every single one of you that I find myself here, at the end of our wandering. All of our lives we have been space gypsies, vagabonds drifting from star to star without a home to call our own, living in hope that we would make it here, to this place, to journey's end. I don't know about any of you, but I will admit now that we are here that I never thought this day would come. It always felt like…a promise." She paused to take in a deep breath. "Every day was spent living in hope. Hope that we would set foot on real earth under a real sky. Now it is so much more than hope. Now it is our home. Just saying those words sends a thrill through every inch of my body," Jorie said as applause rippled around the arc. She rammed the spearpoint of the flagpole into the ground. The flag rippled out in the wind. It was the first time any of the crews had seen it. There was a moment that seemed almost suspended in time as they looked at it and realized it was different, and then murmurs broke out, whispers racing around the crowd.

Jorie raised her hand to silence them.

"Today marks the beginning of a new dawn for our people, but we should never stop living in hope, so in the spirit of remembering, and in honor of every one who set out on the journey from Earth, I name this settlement Basecamp Hope so that we might always live in hope." Again applause rippled around the arc. Jorie smiled, lowering her head slightly.

"You will have noticed the slight change to our sovereign flag. It is in the spirit of courage shown by our forefathers on that day so long ago when they first set foot upon the *Beacon* and the sense of joyous optimism we all feel for tomorrow that we've taken the best of the old and added to it the single-most important symbol of hope our people have ever known, the star of Tau Ceti. This," she said, holding the flag out for all to see, properly, "is our flag, just as this is our land." She looked around her, letting them have a moment to think about what she was really saying, before stepping away from the flag. She didn't want it to dominate the moment—there was more at stake here than changing a flag. It was about owning the future and taking control of their own lives. Up until now they had always been a part of the old Earth, even if those ties had stretched remarkably thin. Now they were truly striking out on their own. Planting a flag was just the first and most obvious symbol. There would be more in the days and months to come. But everything had to begin somewhere, in some gesture, and their story truly began here in the planting of this flag, Jorie thought, because up until then they had always been a part of their parents' and their grandparents' and their great grandparents' stories. But from here on it was all theirs. "I believe in every single man, woman and child before me now. I really do." She looked at them one by one, holding their gaze before moving on to the next. "I believe in you. All of you. You are Basecamp Hope. And I am so proud to call you my friends."

"Three cheers for Captain Platt! Three cheers for Hope!" someone in the crowd shouted, and the cry was taken up by nearly four thousand voices.

She beamed at them, letting them shout their hurrahs.

It felt good to be home.

"I won't promise you the future," she said, her voice dropping in volume as the cheers subsided. She squinted up at the sun, and then raised a hand to cover her eyes. The sun. What a wonderful, wonderful thing. "Instead," she continued, "I *will* promise you today. Today we are—"

But Jorie was interrupted by a disturbance at the back of the crowd before she could finish making her promises.

The press of bodies parted. She couldn't see what had caused the consternation among them at first. The scouting party had returned a day early—or at least one of the scouts had. There was no sign of the rest of them.

And that, by itself, was bad news.

She recognized the man moving unsteadily through the crowd. Nathan Bandurski. He was one of Sendy Montoir's men from the *Conquistador*. He didn't look good. He lurched from foot to foot barely seeming to keep himself upright. No one reached out to help him, though. The crowd shrank back from him as though he was contagious.

Jorie took a single step toward the scout, dreading the delivery of his message, whatever it might be. They'd been through so much, couldn't they just have today?

By the time Bandurski staggered the last few steps into the center of the circle every last ounce of his strength was spent. He collapsed to his knees. He was trying to say something. His mouth was working over and over but nothing was coming. He reached out for Jorie and then pitched forward onto his face.

Jorie crouched down beside him.

She checked the thick vein at his throat for a pulse. He was still alive, but looking at him it was hard to believe he would remain that way for long.

Sendy Montoir crouched down beside her.

They were both well aware that every eye was on them and that this was the first real test of her leadership since the two crews had joined forces.

"What's wrong with him?" Sendy asked.

They moved him gently into the recovery position. "Give him some air," Jorie barked at the encroaching crowd. "Someone get a stretcher, we need to get him up into the medical bay. Now! Move!" She tilted his head, making sure his airways were free of obstruction. "Does he have any pre-existing conditions? Epilepsy? Anything that could explain what's going on? Think!"

Sendy shook her head.

Bandurski looked like hell. He had blisters around his lips, and a rash around the curve of his right eye socket. He couldn't speak.

"Has he been ill recently?"

Sendy shook her head, about to say no, but then remembered the general feelings of queasiness that had afflicted some of them as they came out of lightspeed. "Maybe."

"What do you mean, maybe?"

"When we came into orbit, several of the crew reported migraines, strange muscular aches, and nausea. The medics prescribed painkillers and stimulants to keep them going. I'd need to check sickbay records to see if Bandurski was one of them."

"Then do it," Jorie snapped.

Sendy didn't need telling twice.

Bandurski opened his eyes. His lips moved.

Jorie couldn't make out what he was trying to say.

She leaned in closer, pressing her ear to his lips.

He seemed to be saying—or trying to say—the same two words over and over. "Help me."

2

218 years since the Beacon's *departure from Earth.*
1 year after its arrival at Tau Ceti.

THERE WERE BETTER WAYS to die, Jurudu thought, looking out of the window at the gathering mob. He could feel the violence simmering down there. It would only take a single spark and all hell would break loose. That was all it ever took. One spark. One voice. One miserable little *thing*. Events lined up like a chain of dominos, each seemingly unrelated and yet part of an elaborate pattern that came together to make the here-and-now as the here-and-now could only ever be. One change in the position of these metaphorical dominos, one subtle difference in the outcome of an event or the interplay of an action, reaction or interaction and the world doesn't end.

Only one.

"That way lies madness," Jurudu said.

His executioner didn't argue.

They were in the Presidential Suite of the Governance Tower, in the room where until a few minutes ago Elé Jurudu had ruled the world.

The protestors down there in the People's Plaza carried placards and banners that all demanded variations of the same thing: GIVE US OUR FUTURE BACK!

Their future!

It had always been about *their* future.

Always.

Still, if Juno Lynn did his job properly he would be dead soon, and where would that leave them? Alone, that was where. He struggled to keep his rage in check. Now more than ever Jurudu needed to maintain his focus. He had not lived this long by giving in to his base emotions and letting them rule him. Fear, anger, sadness, joy, disgust, surprise, they had no place in his world. He needed to think. And to think he needed a clear head.

These were *his* people.

He was their President.

Everything he had ever done had been for their greater good. The Austerity Program to conserve dwindling resources, the Youth Services Act that brought in conscription to the armed forces for all boys aged sixteen, and the welfare services for girls of the same age, giving them a chance to be useful and learn a trade, giving something back. The Freedom of Information Act, which protected them from the worst of what was happening out there. All of it, every last law and bylaw and speech he had ever made had been for them.

But that was all forgotten now.

History turned on small moments and in this case it could not have been much smaller: a piece of floating ice.

Jurudu sighed. It was not a contented sound.

Ice.

The grander the plans you made, the more Fate delighted in laughing in your face.

He pressed his forehead up against the bulletproof glass. It felt painfully cold against his skin.

Ice.

There was no escaping it.

Jurudu wanted to break something.

He would just have to satisfy himself by killing someone instead.

He would have liked to walk up behind Lynn, wrap his hands around the man's scrawny neck and snap it like a twig, but that wasn't an option.

He was at a disadvantage.

He needed to be ruthless. Calculated and cunning. Brute force was for lesser men. He was Jurudu. He had an audience. He would offer them death as entertainment and turn it around on them to put the fear of…not God…something far more mortal, and far more vengeful, into them…the fear of him. It would be good to remind them what he was capable of.

Jurudu ground his teeth together.

He rolled his head on his neck, stretching the muscles.

Jurudu hadn't seen the message from the *Conquistador* when it was originally broadcast on the sub-ether network. He should have been the first to see it. People in his staff should have seen it. People in the Communications Division that he trusted should have stopped it from being broadcast. That was their job. Instead the scientist's scaremongering had gone out unedited. The level of incompetence he found him-self surrounded with was dizzying at times. It was supposed to have been his moment of glory. He was meant to have been able to go on the live-feed and offer a brand new world to his people. But there was no Paradise out there, at least not at Tau Ceti. Only Hell. To compound things, the geniuses at Com-ms couldn't find the source of the signal, so they couldn't kill it. Meaning it played over and over and over. They claimed the man behind it was a ghost. That was his identity on the sub-ether: Ghost. It was a cruel joke, and for once it was on him.

People didn't need to know that all of their suffering and the years of privation had been in pursuit of Hell.

They should have been protected from that.

That was why he was there, to shoulder the burden and worry and grieve for them so that they could go about their day-to-day lives without ever grasping how bad things truly were.

But instead Andre Pellar's last message—with that sickening image of Karl Vinton slack-jawed, dead-eyed and slumped in the Captain's Chair—had gone viral. Where he had promised them mountains and lush green pastures and crystal blue lakes there was billowing smoke, there was broil-ing lava, hurricane winds and spumes of magma. The truth had made a liar of him.

So now the protestors were out there with their banners and their clever slogans, making a fool out of him. He saw dozens of placards bearing Pellar's last words: THIS PLACE IS HELL! They could just as easily have meant Earth as Sarbras. Hell was Hell, with lava, with ice, or just frozen in disap-pointment and good intentions.

He had never felt so utterly lost.

This was not how it was meant to be.

He was a better man than this.

He had made tough choices, but each one had been made for the good of his people. But that didn't matter now. They had turned on him. They would never believe another word that came out of his mouth.

And all because of a lump of ice floating stupidly up there in the sky.

It was all part of some great cosmic joke, it had to be, with Fate the greatest comedian ever to take the stage orchestrating his humiliation.

The impact of the collision had been just enough to alter the trajectory of the *Conquistador* probe's re-entry, and from that moment on the rest was history.

Jurudu sucked in a huge lungful of air and held it, counting out the seconds until he couldn't hold it anymore. What happened next was inevitable. He *had* to exhale. He couldn't hold his breath forever. There was a lesson there. He couldn't hold this damned world together forever, either. He had to let go of it. People got the lives they deserved, not the ones he wanted for them.

Even so, it was hard to accept that something so utterly pointless was to blame. He looked down at the ants marching beneath him, all of them so eager to tear his world apart and because of something so...so...*mundane*. It was hardly fair! After everything he had done, after all of the personal sacrifices he had made to serve his people, and his struggles to bring them this far, the risks he had taken on their behalf to give them their freedom in the first place...*this* was his reward?

Jurudu slammed his clenched fist against the window.

The glass shivered under the impact, but was never in any danger of breaking. It was a long way down. He wouldn't survive the fall. Not that he could fall. The windows were hermetically sealed. Nothing was getting in or out of them. Jurudu could have fired a dozen high velocity shells at the glass and followed up with a battering ram, he still wouldn't have been able to hurl himself into the heavens waiting on the other side. Years of paranoia had effectively driven him to build his own prison. There was one door in, one door out.

There was no other way out of the Presidential Office.

He was a good man. He didn't deserve this.

The probe *should* have fallen at the designated landing site. A military base close to the capitol had been prepared, the coordinates were hardwired into the probe's circuitry. And as soon as the probe had come into scanner range they had plotted the course, mapped out the trajectory, and were sure to within a tenth of a mile where it was coming down...right up until it hit that lump of ice.

It could have broken up under the stresses of re-entry. That would have saved him all of this trouble, but no, it had to come down intact. There were 139 million square miles of ocean that could have made all of his problems go away. That was just one more reason he was sure that Fate was enjoying itself. It landed in a place the insurgents still called the Cradle of Civilization.

That was where Ghost had recovered it.

Ghost was not some backwater primitive driven by suspicion and superstition. That, too, might have saved him, if the man had decided to worship the thing that had fallen from the sky as some sort of gift from God. But he knew exactly what he had in his hands, and how to best use it. The man must have hated Jurudu. That could be the only answer that could account for his actions, but what Jurudu couldn't understand was what *he* had ever done to him to earn such enmity?

Rebel, freedom fighter, terrorist, it was all a game of semantics with these people, he realized now. Leader, hero, man of the people, dictator, oppressor, murderer, there was a never-ending list of ways to twist words to suit the message you wanted to deliver and now he was on the receiving end of it. The insurgents were hell-bent on destabilizing his government at any cost. They didn't care how much damage they caused to the lives of the common man and woman.

Once Ghost had decoded the message he made it his crusade to broadcast the truth.

And, as it always seemed to be these days, the message was bleak, but he didn't think for a minute that it was the truth.

Jurudu was a lot of things but he wasn't a fool; there was something about Pellar's recording that just felt wrong. As someone intimately familiar with shaping the facts to fit his needs, Jurudu recognized the same sort of economies at play in Pellar's little speech. But he had to admit that Karl Vinton was a nice touch. Theatrical. However it begged an entirely new line of questioning; why show only Vinton? Why not the others? Why not pan the camera around the bridge and bring home the whole shocking truth—unless it wasn't the truth?

Jurudu was well aware of the scientist's relationship with Renee Sinha, the militant protestor, and by extension her affiliations to the group that had sabotaged Chambers-Osawa's original tests. The fact that she had chosen to save him meant that Pellar had remained under suspicion, even without her confession, hence his promotion to head the Tau Ceti project. It wasn't a reward. Far from it, it was a case of keep your friends close and your enemies much *much* closer.

He thought of Pellar, leaning in close to the camera urging them to give up on Sarbras, and again found himself doubting the truth of his own eyes. If the faster-than-light drives were so fundamentally flawed why was Pellar unaffected? Why wasn't he sprawled out like Vinton, glassy eyed and frothing at the mouth? It made no logical sense. Nothing about the broadcast did when it was examined properly. It appealed on a purely emotive level. That was what made it such a brilliant move by the traitor, Pellar. The man may have spent his days sneaking about like some worthless weasel, peopling the *Conquistador* with blood relatives of the Beacon's original traitors, and thinking Jurudu was clueless to his plots and schemes. Give a man enough rope and he will inevitably hang himself. Pellar's treason was a matter of record now. Unfortunately, it had been far more effective—spectacularly so—than the scientist could have possibly dreamed, and all because of a little piece of ice.

Andre Pellar would come to regret that.

Of course, the end had begun long before Andre Pellar's damned transmission. The roots were already growing in the days leading up to the rebel bombing of Complex Alpha. That was five years ago. And why? Because of some messed up loyalty to the so-called pioneers who had fled the planet at its time of greatest need? It made Jurudu physically sick to think of the way these people were idolized. They were cowards and traitors; it was as simple as that. They had bled the world dry and then fled it. How could that ever be heroic? The heroes were the ones left behind. The ones who lived on a dying world for two centuries, adapting, surviving, making the best of it; those were the heroes.

He took some small satisfaction now in knowing that the *Beacon*'s two-century-long flight had delivered them to a world of fire. It was poetic. They deserved to burn for what they had done.

He saw smoke on the horizon.

It was the Beta Site, ablaze. It had been burning all night. There were other fires out there, too. He could see the smoke stacks rising into the sky. On the banks of monitors that surrounded his room there were similar images. All across the world—his world—things were burning. They had started out by attacking everything involved in the space program, but once they'd got a hunger for violence they turned their attention to anything that reminded them of Jurudu himself.

Couldn't these idiots grasp that such wanton destruction only hurt themselves?

No, of course they couldn't.

They lived in a myopic world of self self self. They didn't see beyond it. They didn't see the huge mosaic that was everyone's lives all interlinked and interconnected and interdependent. He did. He saw them all, each and every one of them and all of the strands that linked them. He understood how by destroying Complex Alpha and the prototype FTL drives they'd set their own futures back by almost a decade and prolonged the Austerity Program. It was a logical chain of cause and effect. Because of that single act of terrorism the bright new dawn labored on in darkness. But none of the rebels would ever stand up and admit that their actions had caused five more years of suffering for the common people, would they? None of them would say sorry there's no food for you because of us, would they?

No, they wouldn't, because they were cowards.

It didn't suit them to own their actions.

Jurudu was expected to shoulder the burden and take the blame for everything they did, too. It was up to him to be the hero his people needed. It had always been the same way. Whatever else they might say about him, no one could ever claim Elé Jurudu had shirked his responsibilities. He was a man bound by duty, and had the most metaphorically broad shoulders of any man who had ever lived. He could bear a world on them.

The end always had a beginning.

This one had begun with a lie.

That was the only thing Jurudu could think.

Someone with a grudge against him must have infiltrated his command and doctored the original Tau Ceti probe findings. He had always known he had enemies, he just hadn't appreciated the long game they had been playing, or how dirty they were prepared to play it, and as a result had failed to protect himself from it.

Those original images haunted him now.

Perhaps Ghost had been responsible for that creative vandalism, too? It was possible, wasn't it? Or was that just paranoia talking?

He was being just like them. He needed someone to blame, too.

Pellar's broadcast and the truth of Sarbras had led to more disturbances. The worst of them still burned brightly inside Jurudu. He bore the scars of it on the left side of his face. It had been a week after Pellar had shown the world Hell. Just one week. This beautiful sad-faced woman at the back of the crowd had pushed her way toward the front cradling what everyone thought was a baby. They made way for her. It wasn't uncommon for women to want Jurudu to bless their children, there were people out there who still believed in him. But not this mother. Her baby was dead and its body had been packed with explosives.

Jurudu had been very lucky that day.

Others hadn't.

It had gone out on the live-feed.

He could defend his actions until he was blue in the face, it wouldn't have mattered. These people didn't want to see the good he had done. They ignored the advances in healthcare, how he had seen them through famine only a few years ago, investing precious millions in finding alternate food sources, the same food sources that were the only reason they were still alive after the extinction of the bees. They didn't care that medical advances developed under his rule had meant they survived an influenza pandemic that had threated to decimate the young and old alike. No, they only saw the hardships his Austerity Program necessitated, and blamed him for the life-expectancy decrease. They didn't mention the new plagues sent to try them, the new famines, or the fact that the Four Horsemen had been riding roughshod across the Earth for years now.

They genuinely hated him, and it didn't matter what he did, what sacrifices he made, nothing would change that. It was the kind of hate that burns bright in black souls, that was the only explanation for what had happened. He bore the scars of their hate. They were a constant reminder that the road to Hell was paved with good intentions.

It was all coming undone.

They were like ants down there, so small, and yet so full of purpose. They spread out through the People's Plaza. He could see patterns in their movement. Precision. It wasn't random. Despite the seeming chaos, it was anything but chaotic. Their rage was driven by a desire to see a new kind of order. Jurudu watched as protestors spread a sheet out between them. He could barely read it because of the height and the angle, but as the wind picked up and bullied it, the sheet twisted and he saw what it said: YOU STOLE TOMORROW! WE WANT TODAY!

There were comfortably fifteen thousand demonstrators crushed into the Plaza. Fifteen thousand people. It broke his heart. Protestors had already broken into the Presidential Tower and were on their way up to his office. It was only a matter of time.

History was washing its hands of him.

"All I ever did was offer them hope," Jurudu told his reflection in the bulletproof glass. "When did that become a crime?"

"You think too much of yourself, Jurudu," his executioner said. "It's been a long time since you gave anyone anything." The man sat in his high-backed leather chair. He had a gun resting on his thigh. It wasn't an ordinary gun. It was the kind they used to kill livestock. A bolt gun. He hadn't even got the courtesy to threaten Jurudu with it.

The executioner's name was Juno Lynn. He was low down on the totem pole of the Surveillance & Security Bureau. An interrogator. He was also a traitor.

If he had a year to recount all of the crimes Lynn had perpetrated he wouldn't have had enough time to list even half of them. The man was the kind of vile scum you needed to protect your country from outside forces; no ethics, no moral code, no qualms when it came to inflicting pain to get what he wanted, because the ends always justified the means, and now here he was serving as the people's judge, jury and executioner. So be it. Jurudu wasn't afraid to die.

But he wasn't finished living just yet.

He had known this moment was coming.

He was prepared.

You didn't survive as long as Jurudu had without planning for all eventualities, no matter how unpleasant they might seem. Other men might put off thinking about death, preferring to believe they were blessed with some form of temporary immortality, but not Jurudu. He had always known he was going to die, and had embraced the knowledge because it made him stronger. It allowed him to plan. There were contingencies in place to assure death would find Jurudu on his own terms. There would always be exceptions, of course, things he couldn't control, but even then he laid down plans for how events should play out.

He turned away from the window as the great bronze statue of him teetered on its huge plinth. It would fall soon enough, he didn't need to see it. The symbolism of it wasn't lost on him.

"Shall we get this over with then?"

"In good time, Jurudu." Lynn looked at his watch as though making a point. "Do you hear that?" He cocked his head, listening to something Jurudu couldn't hear. "They are coming for you." The executioner's smile was cruel. "They're inside already. There's no one to stop them. I made sure of that. All of the security in the world won't save you now. Every barrier from here down to the ground has been neutralized. There's just you and me now, Jurudu. Two old friends. Does that frighten you? It should. I know you better than you know yourself, old man. I know all of your lies because I've been at your side the whole time listening to them. Hell, I've even spouted a few on your behalf."

"I am not scared of you."

"You should be."

"You talk too much. Every time you open your mouth I am reminded of how inconsequential you are."

"I'm the man who killed the Great Jurudu. I'd say that makes me pretty important."

"Not yet you're not."

"Think of this as your confessional," Lynn said, as though he hadn't been listening to a word Jurudu had said. "Talk to the people out there, cleanse yourself." The executioner motioned toward the live-feed cameras. "Let me give you some things to start you off: tell them why you've grown fat while they've gone hungry. Tell them how you've controlled everything they've ever seen and everything they think they know of the world. Tell them how the Surveillance & Security Bureau has been listening in to their telephone calls and intercepting their mail for years. Tell them that those accidents that befell loved ones might not have been accidents at all, but murders 'for the greater good' carried out in your name. Tell them why it was so important for you to throw good money chasing bad dreams of space while they lost their homes and livelihoods and queued up in the streets, trading Austerity Coupons for bread and scraps of meat. Tell them everything, because they deserve to hear it from your lying mouth, Mister President. But tell them *quickly* because I'll be brutally honest with you, I'm bored of hearing the sound of your voice and my trigger finger is itchy."

"Is this how you want it to end, Juno?"

"I want it to end with you dead, Mister President. The rest of it doesn't matter in the slightest. But, you're right, perhaps you should be on your knees? Let the world see you penitent, broken at the last."

"If it makes you happy," Jurudu said, and sank slowly to his knees and put his hands behind his head. It was meant to make him look submissive. Beaten. "There. I'm kneeling. But I am not ashamed. I have done no wrong. Everything I have ever done has been with the best interests of my people in mind." This was the moment of truth, where risk and reward came together.

"I think that's up to the world to decide, don't you?" There was a glibness to Juno Lynn's tone that Jurudu really did not like. The man needed to be brought down a peg or two. He would be humbled soon enough. Jurudu closed his eyes. It appeared to be the act of a truly penitent man—either that or a coward who could not face death. He was neither. When he opened them again it would all be over. "Is that it? No last words for the sake of posterity? Speak now or forever hold your peace. The world is watching, Mister President. And there's nowhere left for you to hide." Lynn looked toward the live-feed camera. Every screen in the world would be tuned to this moment.

It would do them good to be reminded why he had lived quite so long, and why his enemies had not.

He lowered his head, and said the word.

And the word was, "Sorry."

Lynn sneered. "Is that it? The very last word of the Great Jurudu?"

"You were expecting more?" He didn't look up. Sorry was the one word that would never knowingly pass his lips, making it the perfect word to trigger the safeguards of his room. He could never have allowed himself to be taken alive. Too much of the world's infrastructure was keyed in to his voice print and his biometrics. The suicide option had just saved his life. Juno Lynn should have known that he wouldn't go easily, but then, hubris had killed better men than him.

"Well, it's just a little...disappointing." Lynn flinched as the poison-tipped dart punched into the lumbar region of his spine, delivering the lethal dose directly into his spinal fluid. His face contorted, his jaw twisted as he bit through his tongue. It was not pretty.

"No, as last words go *that* was just a little disappointing," Jurudu said. He opened his eyes.

Lynn stared back at him. There was still some life in there. He could see the horror of realization behind the eyes as they glazed over. Blood dribbled down his chin. It was always good when they understood why they had died.

Jurudu rose to his feet.

He took the time to straighten his clothes.

He looked directly at the live-feed camera. "My people," he said, smiling warmly now, the benevolent dictator forgiving the sins of his folk. "And you *are* still my people, believe me. It would appear that this little insurrection has failed. I forgive you, because I understand your grief. I forgive you, because tomorrow is another day, the future, and everything we have ever been through together has been about tomorrow. But I have a message for those of you who took up arms against me, those of you who burned *my* cities; I do not forgive you. I will hunt you to the ends of the Earth. I will find you. And I *will* kill you for your treason. You have my word on that. And despite what you may have been told by these liars, I have never failed to deliver on my promises." He looked meaningfully at the corpse of Juno Lynn in his chair, then back at the live-feed camera lens. "This is Elé Jurudu, your President, and you have my word that peace *will* be restored in short order. My government is aware of who the traitors are. We have been monitoring their activities for quite some time now, waiting for the moment to shut them down, whilst remaining hopeful that they would come to understand the error of thinking by themselves. Sadly it was not to be. Even as I speak, there are agents from the Surveillance & Security Bureau on their way to apprehend them. They will be re-educated. To the rest of you, the decent, loyal majority, I urge you to return to your homes and return to your place of work in the morning. In that way we can help each other. Together we will make tomorrow happen today, that is my promise to you."

With that, he killed the live-feed.

It was all bravado, face saving. But it would not hurt for them to remember him as a man to be feared.

He had no intention of lingering in the office, surrounded by the trappings of the life he had to leave behind. There was no room for sentimentality. The next hour was going to be all about survival.

He stripped the executioner quickly, trading clothes with him. It was a simple subterfuge and it wouldn't hold up to close scrutiny, but from a distance it could buy him a few vital seconds and right now every second was a precious commodity.

Jurudu looked around the office for one final time, looking at the exquisite works of art he had amassed, at the things of great beauty he would never see again, because when he set foot out of this room there was no going back. He'd always known this day would come. It hung over him like some sword wielded by Damocles himself. It had hung over him for so long he didn't even resent its presence anymore. It was just a fact of life, like shitting, it just happened, and you never talked about it. He resisted the temptation to claim something, a memento from the treasures around the room, because every additional ounce was an added burden and would bring additional strain to bear on the journey he was about to take.

He closed the door and stepped out into the antechamber.

Lynn hadn't been lying.

A corpse manned his secretary's desk. She had been felled by Lynn's bolt gun. There was a hole in the side of her head where the metal bolt had punched through.

There were three more bodies slumped on the other side of the waiting room. One of them wore a hat. Jurudu had already discovered he wasn't above stealing a dead man's clothes, so he put the hat on and pulled it down so it shaded his eyes. He was fatter than people realized, but not fat enough that it could have passed for the distended belly of malnutrition. It was the belly of a contented man who hadn't starved for anything, not even for a single day of his life. It would give him away, but there was nothing he could do about it.

Jurudu left the waiting room. There were three passageways, each seeming to stretch on endlessly thanks to a trick of the architectural design. He could hear them now. Their heavy footsteps echoed up the stairwell. They were much closer than he would have liked.

As he reached the bank of elevators the fire door burst open and the first of the rebels came through. There were three men behind him. The sixty stories had taken their toll. They were the only people in the world he knew for sure could not have seen him kill Juno Lynn. He didn't try and hide. There was nowhere he could, and any sort of hesitation would have sold him out. Thinking on his feet, Jurudu looked back over his shoulder and said, "He's in there with Lynn."

"Come on," the first man through the door barked. "We don't want to miss the bastard getting what's coming to him."

Jurudu kept his head down as they rushed past him, then he pushed open the fire door and slipped through into the stairwell.

The second lot of intruders were two flights below him, coming up fast.

He started to climb.

Jurudu was laboring hard by the time he reached the eightieth floor, and he still had nineteen more to go to the roof and the high-altitude shuttle waiting on the helipad. His thighs burned, and his calf muscles trembled from the strain. He could feel his shinbones pressing out against the skin. He used the handrail to haul himself up another two steps at a time. His ragged breathing drowned out the purr of the air vents. Rage, like vengeful wraiths, haunted the stairwell behind him. They had found Juno Lynn. He looked down over the rails. The bottom was so far away he couldn't see it anymore. Jurudu's head swam with something akin to vertigo as he leaned out. He hauled himself back, looking up to give his balance a moment to settle. They were still twenty stories below, so they could find whatever they wanted, he didn't care. So long as he could make it to the top before they closed the gap between them he was free.

Ten stories.

Eight.

Five.

The catcalls and baying of the witch-hunt grew louder by the minute. It filled the stairs, racing up to the roof and echoing back down at him. Jurudu gasped and grunted, forcing himself on. On the next landing he risked leaning out over the railing and looking down. He could see flashes of color from sleeves and clenched fists chasing up after him. The gap between them was considerably shorter now, and with him in their sights the mob had found its second wind, making the climb two and three stairs at a time.

Three.

Two.

Jurudu doubled over, hands on knees, breathing hard. He was spent. Eighteen flights of stairs were murder, but he dug deep, finding the reserves of strength he needed to force himself up another one. Reduced to basics, it was that or die and his determination to *live* drove him on.

He stumbled on the next rise, missing the step and losing his footing. He fell face first, landing on his outstretched hands. He took the weight of the fall on his forearm. It was a miracle the bone didn't break. He lay there for a second, gasping and listening to the sounds of pursuit. No matter how badly he wanted to, Jurudu couldn't lie there. He forced himself back to his feet and stumbled-ran as best he could to the next landing.

He was one flight from the top.

He needed to slow them down.

Jurudu looked around for something that could buy him time.

The one obvious thing was staring him right in the face: a huge red fire axe.

He tugged it free from the wall mount, hefted it against his shoulder and brought it slamming down into the glass casing that housed the fire alarm. He chipped the splinters and jagged edges of glass away with the butt of the axe handle, and then reached in and tugged down the lever. Seconds later the sprinklers kicked in throughout the huge tower and the claxons wailed into life. They were deafening, and only made more maddening by the confines of the stairway.

The tower was constructed in stages, and each stage could be sealed off in the event of fire or other threat. That was just common sense. Every fourth floor there were huge blast doors that isolated the stairwells. The design was intended to deny the rising flames of oxygen and suffocate them rather than allowing them to rage on up and up the innards of the tower. But it served a secondary purpose, adding physical barriers to impede any intruder's ascent.

Jurudu started to run, but legs like jelly betrayed him before he was even halfway up the final flight of stairs. He stumbled, and tried desperately to stand again, knowing he only had seconds to make it up to the top—the ninety-ninth floor—before the blast doors closed isolating the roof and trapping him in no man's land with nothing between him and the baying mob.

There was a sharp piston-burst of compressed air that came a second before the doors slammed shut.

Jurudu threw himself through the gap, barely dragging his feet clear before the doors could amputate them.

He lay on his back, his feet flat against the blast doors, safe, gasping and laughing, as adrenaline surged through his body.

He felt so incredibly *alive*.

He missed this feeling.

He had been cooped up in that damned office for too long. He was a man of action. This stuff was in his blood. It was what his heart beat for.

Jurudu climbed the final steps to the roof door and placed his hand flat on the ident-pad. This was the moment of truth. If Lynn was as good as he thought he was, he'd have over-ridden security and made sure Jurudu's biometrics had been wiped from the system. That's what he would have done in Lynn's place. But then Lynn had been arrogant enough to sit in his chair and play out his little game of poke the bear instead of just getting the job done. Arrogance bred mistakes.

The door opened.

Lynn hadn't thought beyond what would happen if he failed in his execution attempt, he had simply assumed he would be the one walking away from that room and there'd be no need to wipe Jurudu from the system. The man's lacka-daisical attention to detail had saved Jurudu's life.

Jurudu stepped out onto the roof.

The winds were fierce, pushing and bullying him as he ran head-down, crouching low, toward the ramp and the waiting high-altitude shuttle. The helipad was so far above the Plaza he couldn't hear anything apart from the wind.

He rushed toward the shuttle.

It looked like a giant ant crouched on six legs, with a bul-bous head with the Presidential Seal emblazoned on it. The blacked out windows were like multifaceted eyes and antenna sprouted out of the shuttle's "head" like mandibles. The gull-wing door in the side of the hull was open.

Jurudu cast one last lingering look back at the door to be sure that no one was following him, and then ducked slightly as he clambered in beneath the gull-wing.

There were banks of seating on either side of a central aisle. The shuttle could comfortably seat fifty people.

It was empty.

He checked the cockpit.

There was no sign of the pilot or the rest of the crew.

It didn't matter. A monkey could fly this thing. Jurudu tripped the circuit to close the door, and then buckled himself into the pilot's seat. Placing his palm flat against the console, he powered up the sub-light engines, giving them a moment to gather power before adjusting the vertical takeoff boosters and taking the shuttle up. The sensors came online. The black tint of the reactive oil film retracted from the windshield. It provided extra protection from the sun's rays and toughened the glass up as pressures on it increased the higher it flew.

For all of his bluster, Lynn was right about one thing: there was nowhere in this world left for him to hide. Jurudu had no interest in living in a bolt hole underground like a mole, surviving hand-to-mouth, or spending his final years on the run, moving from settlement to settlement and avoiding any cities for fear of being recognized. He was Jurudu. He had nothing to be ashamed about. He had simply been outmaneuvered by his opponent. The battle wasn't over. Not while there was breath in his lungs. But for now, what other alternatives were there? He wasn't prepared to enter surgery and doubted very much there was a doctor good enough with a knife to change his face, and loose enough when it came to morals to do the operation, and who couldn't just as easily be bought by the men looking for him. He could, of course, kill the plastic surgeon, but that would only lead to an investigation. There would always be tracks to follow. His new face would come out eventually. Fate was like that.

Everything rested upon how good a judge of liar he was—and Jurudu believed he was the very best. Only time would tell.

The rooftop lurched away beneath him as the shuttle banked and rose, taking him up.

The ascent took fifteen minutes.

The roar of the shuttle's engines filled the cockpit. He killed the ground-to-air voicecom because the constant bleating of the woman on the other end repeating over and over that he wasn't authorized for takeoff was annoying. In another life he had flown combat aircraft. The shuttle was cumbersome and unresponsive, and remarkably low-tech in comparison to those old fighters he used to fly, but the controls were still familiar enough for him to feel in complete control of the ascent.

He tapped in the coordinates for the orbital manufacturing yard.

The *Conquistador* had always been intended as the first ship of many to be built up there. But even with a hundred thousand of them they couldn't have traded Earth for Sarbras; that was the mathematical truth behind the dream. It was only ever going to be a new life for a select few. Even if that "few" equated to a hundred thousand people, it would take over thirty years to shuttle them on the *Conquistador*. A dozen ships would have meant almost half a million of the Earth's inhabitants could have been relocated in that time. It was a pipe dream. But then, it had never been about relocating people to the distant moon, it had always been about plundering it, bringing its rich resources back here.

No matter how many times he saw it, the vast platforms and cranes of the manufacturing yard set against a backdrop of empty sky really was an inspiring sight; the pinnacle of human ingenuity and engineering they called it, and with good reason. It was like a giant city floating almost three hundred miles above the Earth's surface. It had a patchwork look to its construction with hundreds of pre-constructed pressurized modules cobbled together to form the bulkhead of the yards, the cranes just gigantic robotic arms manipulated from within these modular living habitats. The yard's assembly cost more than $132 billion, making it more expensive than rebuilding the infrastructure of the entire Asian basin after the most recent earthquakes and floods. It was a city in space. And since the failure of the *Conquistador* it had lain seemingly abandoned, the single greatest folly of his administration.

Seemingly.

On the far side, blocked from satellite feed imagery, a second FTL ship had been built during those months and years the *Conquistador* was constructed, doubling up on many parts orders, drafting across trusted labor. But that was the beauty of the mechanized yard, it didn't require hundreds of men with loose tongues to work on it, just the designer who also served as central programmer and fed the designs to the various machines, and a few trusted engineers to oversee the work, and once it was finished it could be replicated again and again with relative ease building a fleet. Designed to much simpler specifications, the *Inquisitor* was considerably smaller, and made for a crew of fifty men instead of one thousand, her hull compact, and driven by powerfully efficient engines that were less than a third the size of the Chambers-Osawa originals.

A team of ten men had put her together.

Everything about the FTL ship was a refinement on the *Conquistador* template. The plan had been to construct one hundred of the *Inquisitor* class ships, equip them with warheads with nuclear payloads and take them to Sarbras to secure the beachhead Vinton's mission should have established. In his head he imagined one hundred Inquisitors dropping out of lightspeed and the sheer shock their arrival would bring. Any lingering resistance from the Beaconites would have died a miserable death at the sight. Jurudu savored that thought for a moment.

Only one *Inquisitor* class ship had ever been finished, because the news of Tau Ceti's hostile environment and the fatally flawed FTL drive designs had left the program in limbo, but the skeletons of ninety-nine more were in various forms of completion around the yard. It would only take a metaphorical flick of a switch to resume building.

That couldn't be allowed to happen.

They couldn't be allowed to follow him into space. Not now.

As the shuttle neared the landing bays, Jurudu made the final adjustments for docking. The yard loomed nearer. As the angle of his approach altered he saw more and more of the *Inquisitor*-class skeletons visible through the lower crane arms. It was like a mechanized graveyard.

Jurudu brought the shuttle alongside the docking arm, allowing the landing program to bring him in. There was a burst of compressed air behind him as the airlocks sealed a moment later and then the steady stream of breathable air being filtered into the vacuum, balancing out the pressure between the shuttle and the dock. It was an annoyingly slow process, but it made the difference between being torn apart by invisible forces and sprayed across the interior of the docking bay like some abstract blood and guts painting and not. A few minutes quite literally wouldn't kill him. He checked the long-range scanners. There was no sign of pursuit from the ground.

The pressure indicators changed to green.

He killed the shuttle's engines and powered down, then thought better of it, firing them back up. He would need the extra volatility they offered to bring the manufacturing yard down. They whined into life. As he walked through the shuttle to the airlock door at the rear, he thought for a moment that he could feel the shuttle straining at the leash, trying to break free of the docking arm. It was all in his head.

He had two things to do before he boarded the *Inquisitor* and turned his back on Earth forever. The first was to strip the nuclear payload from one of her warheads and plant it at the heart of the yard where all of the spines of the hundreds of platforms and cranes came together, the second was to prime it.

The docking arm was barely lit by emergency lighting. The atmosphere was still being automatically adjusted for his presence. As he raced down along the arm it was still icy cold. His breath frosted in front of his face. There were signs, but every now and then he had to stop and press his face up against the safety glass to peer out and get his bearings. It slowed him down. He kept looking back over his shoulder as though he expected to see someone chasing him, but he was alone up there, just him and the ghosts of the space program.

It didn't take Jurudu long to sabotage the yard.

He knew where to plant the charge so it triggered the yard's "managed collapse"—right in the heart of the web of armatures and cranes, at the fulcrum. The shock from the first explosion would trigger the demolition charges that the architects had built into the design to tear it down should there ever be a need. Now there was a need.

The payload was equipped with timers and impact detonators. Jurudu gave himself fifteen minutes. Even if they came after him now it would do them no good. By the time they arrived there would be nothing left.

He buckled up in the *Inquisitor*'s Captain's chair, placing his hand flat on the console to merge with the ship's bio-computer, assigning himself as the first Captain of planet Earth's first truly long-range interstellar warship, and launched. The coordinates were pre-programmed. Tau Ceti. If, as he suspected, Andre Pellar was lying, he would become the first President of the new world, as was his natural right, and if by some remote chance Pellar had told the truth and Sarbras was this barren Hell he'd shown them, then he would fly on. There would be other planets. The *Inquisitor* was fully equipped, loaded with supplies for fifty men to last the two-month journey. He was one man, the rations would last him twenty-five years, providing they didn't perish first. He wasn't in a hurry.

Behind him, controlled blasts tore the yard apart.

3

218 years since the Beacon's *departure from Earth. Year One: Tau Ceti.*

AWAY FROM THE EYES of others Garber hunkered down over a haunch of meat. He had run the animal down and tore at it now with his bare hands. Blood flecked his teeth and smeared all around his mouth. His eyes were wild. Feral.

✦

Out in the fields beyond the trees and before the mountain peaks Hannon was on his knees at the stream, scooping mouthful after mouthful of water up in his hands. He lapped at it greedily, sucking and swallowing it down. On and on, scooping it out, five minutes, ten, twenty, hand to mouth, hand to mouth. His stomach swelled. His bladder leaked. And on he drank, hand to mouth, hand to mouth even as the urine pooled at his knees. He leaned forward, plunging his head into the stream, mouth open wide, trying desperately to drink it dry even as he toppled forward.

✦

Balham and Saines, two of Sendy's frontier scouts, broke into stores in the middle of the night. The pair of them snuck in under the cover of Sarbras's distant moons. The sky was a long way from black but it was still dark enough that no one could have seen the pair skirt the huge storage bays because they kept tight to the walls where the shadows were thickest. No one would have looked for them, either. Basecamp Hope functioned on trust. No one believed one of their number would steal from another or put the whole colony at risk. They were naïve like that. A man like Elé Jurudu would have said they were idiots like that.

The two men used power bars to break the locks on the huge roller doors and dragged the shutters up just far enough for them to roll under. On the other side of the roller doors it was a glutton's paradise. Hundreds of crates lined the walls, stacked three and four high, arranged according to produce and expiration.

Working their way down the line the pair tore open the supply crates, spilling the ration packs out across the floor and rummaging around in the middle of them like scavengers. When that didn't satisfy them, they broke the vacuum seals on dry ration pouches and scooped handful after handful of dehydrated food out and crunched through them, spitting and swallowing. It didn't help so they turned their attention to the wet food, smearing it across their faces and into their mouths in their desperation to be full.

They crawled around on their hands and knees, pulling down crates, cracking open boxes and tins and pouring out more and more food, their feeding growing more and more frenzied the more they stuffed into their faces. But they quite literally couldn't satisfy the hunger gnawing away at them no matter what they put into their mouths.

The two men shared a look then, and with the telepathy of the insane, scrambled away on their hands and knees toward the livestock pens.

Before they were through the pair of them had spoiled more than a month's worth of food for the entire colony.

✦

Hunger is hunger and it comes in many guises. Some appetites are literal, a craving for meat, a hunger for fresh crisp vegetables, a thirst for a cool quenching drink. Other hungers are no less real, no less physical, no harder to ignore, but purely carnal.

They didn't talk about it, there was no order from on high, it was simply assumed the colony had to grow to survive. It was their duty. The embryos from the birthing chambers were good, but there was a sense of wanting to do it properly, a new world, new life, but not managed, not genetically streamed or manipulated, life brought into life the real way.

They came together, and came together.

It began as sex, but like every other hunger something missing, some lack, amplified it and where the colonists from the *Beacon* found themselves developing the loving relationships that had already formed during the long voyage, looking to build their own dwellings and find that little extra privacy that came with it now they could leave the slowship, while those from the *Conquistador*, suddenly marooned on Sarbras with no way home, thrown together, fear and isolation only amplified by the overriding hungers they quite simply couldn't control, lost themselves in a feast of the flesh.

Slow and smooth was replaced by fast and hard. Two together became three and five and seven as a desperate need replaced any restraint and boundaries came down. It became animalistic.

The colony needed new life.

But still, for a while at least, it remained secretive, even though there was no suggestion that any of them found what they were doing to be *wrong*. They were merely gorging just as the gluttons were gorging. The only difference was when it came to what appetites they couldn't sate.

✦

But Jorie didn't know about any of that.

Not at first. Not until the food supplies were ruined. Then it became an issue for her, but even so she was preoccupied with everything else that needed to be done, but so much that they quite simply couldn't do. They needed to establish the outposts, they needed to establish communication between them, transportation and information highways. It wasn't like some dream where they could simply unroll huge terraforming machines that gave them a world just as they wanted it, or send out drones to cobble together skyscrapers and remake this world in the image of the one their ancestors had left behind. They needed to establish plants to manufacture even the simplest things they were going to need for day-to-day survival. They needed routines. They needed governance.

She didn't simply want to impose her role as Captain of the *Beacon* onto the second ship. And, truth be told, her job was done. The role of the Captain was to see them from Earth to Tau Ceti; now that they were here they needed something completely different. They needed leaders who knew about roads and about farming and plantations and tools and laws and, and, and…What they didn't need was a dictator, and that's what a Captain was. She might start out with the best intentions, but in five years or ten or fifteen what was to say she'd not come to enjoy the power too much? What was to say she wouldn't be just another Jurudu?

No, her first job was to see that a government of equals was democratically elected.

The temptation was to run for a role in this new governing body, but even then, with the mandate of the people, that way lay madness. So many of them, she knew, would vote for her simply because she was Captain of the *Beacon*. She was familiar to them, inherited from Kora Andropolis, and in turn Burton Pellar and so on and so forth back two hundred and some years. She was part of their heritage but they needed a separation of slowship and dry land. An election without her presence would give them that. She would pledge to serve the new government in any capacity they needed from her, ensuring a smooth transition, though.

She had made up her mind.

And then Nathan Bandurski died and everything went to Hell.

✦

Nathan Bandurski slipped into a coma and never regained consciousness.

It took almost four months from his stumbling into the flag planting ceremony until he died. Four months in which they monitored his condition and tried everything they could think of to save him, but nothing they tried had any noticeable effect on his condition. One of the first peculiarities Sendy Montoir noticed about it, was that his body drained the drip-feeds two and three times faster than they were set to run. It didn't matter how they tried to regulate it, his body just demanded more and the machines gave it.

Bandurski wasn't the only one to fall ill.

Over the next three weeks twenty more cases arose, each with varying levels of severity.

The symptoms were peculiar in that more often than not they didn't present themselves as symptoms at all. It began with headaches and nausea in every instance, but quickly subsided into simple increased appetites. Sufferers would carbo-load, gorging themselves on food, and then drink, chugging pint after pint of anything they could down. Sometimes they'd come to the sickbay and ask for help, only to be prescribed stimulants. The stimulants would keep their bodies going until they went into complete shutdown. They were fighting a losing battle. As quickly as they fed the disease it burned through the nutrients and it was only the amphetamines that kept them moving even as their muscle tone degenerated and their organs failed. On a most basic level, they simply couldn't take fuel on fast enough. Their bodies were burning up.

The medics in the sickbay poked and prodded and ran the gamut of tests on the living and the dead, but couldn't come up with a single physical thing wrong with any of the victims. Not a one. Which made the fact that they were dying all the more confusing. Sendy stayed with them, making it a personal project because they were her people. Every last one of them. That was the only thing they knew for sure—the illness, whatever it was, was confined to the travelers who had made the trip to Tau Ceti on the *Conquistador*.

And soon enough they were left with a single conclusion, a unifying factor: the only thing they had in common was that they had all traveled faster than light.

After that realization the medics started calling it Light Sickness, but they didn't really know what that meant. Not yet, at least.

Sendy studied every scrap of information she could find on the crew, on their habits, on what linked them and why certain people seemed more susceptible than others. On average they lasted less than two months after they started vomiting. Some lasted longer, but they were the exception. And there was nothing she or anyone else could do for them. She compared their charts against the travelers from the *Beacon*, looking for anything, any single difference that could account for what was happening to the others, but nothing jumped out at her. Nothing said: *this, look, this is it!*

Two of her crew died of water poisoning long before the Light Sickness itself could finish them.

Sendy Montoir had never felt so helpless in her life.

Reports came back to Basecamp Hope from the outposts: Light Sickness had reached them as well, so it wasn't contained to Hope. But neither was it some sweeping contagion. That confused her. It didn't grip them like a pandemic and cull their number, it spread slowly and resolutely through the one-thousand-strong crew of the *Conquistador*. She knew that meant her time would come. She accepted that. But without being able to isolate what was wrong they were never going to be able to develop a vaccine. That was harder to accept.

A thousand people were counting on her finding the answer, but Sendy felt like she had barely begun to grasp the question never mind work out any sort of answer to it.

Andre Pellar never left her side, even when he started to complain of nausea and light-headedness. He was there, sweat streaming down his temples, hands trembling as he tabbed through the datascreens, studying the results, poring over the blood tests and the tissue samples and everything else they had to hand, trying to enforce his scientist's rationale and discipline onto the problem as though it was simply a structural puzzle to be unraveled.

Pellar talked her through it in a different way, stressing that the body was a machine, a machine that was every bit as complicated as the FTL drives he'd constructed, and when it broke down, just like the FTL drives, it could be repaired. There was an innocence to his logic that appealed to her, but it was more his stubborn refusal to be beaten that drew her back to his side again and again.

They were lovers now.

It had been a natural development of their friendship, and the sheer amount of time they spent together at close quarters, but the things they had shared in Vinton's room had cemented the union. They both knew that. He was the saddest man she had ever met, but so very noble in that sadness. He was a good man. That was the easiest way of defining him, not that anyone could be defined in so few words. What they shared was physical. It didn't go beyond that need, and on that level at least they could both deal with it. He had truly loved his girlfriend, Renee Sinha. The brutality of her murder at the hands of Karl Vinton was still hard for him to accept, but beyond that it was proving almost impossible for him to get over. The pain was ingrained on his soul, and right alongside it, survivor's guilt. She was dead, he wasn't, and as he told it, she'd died because she'd saved his life.

Andre threw himself into his work and erected barriers around his heart that meant even being his friend was hard, too. The first time they had made love he had left in the middle of the night, weeping. She had gone to find him. That was when he had explained about Renee saving him from the Alpha Complex explosion. It wasn't difficult to put all the pieces together after that. They had sat together, not touching, but far more intimate in those long dark hours than they had been only a few hours before when he had been inside her.

The sex changed, though. The sicker he became, the more desperate it became. She noticed it. How could she not? It was addictive, but there was something unhealthy about his appetites. He would try to be tender afterwards, but something in him was broken and she couldn't fix it.

But it wasn't until he started vomiting that Sendy Montoir realized she was in love with him.

✦

There were three patients in the sickbay now: Benitez, Vaughan and Burke. All three of them were fading fast and without a miracle would join the death list within a matter of days.

"Let's look at Bandurski's results again," she said, and for the umpteenth time they went back to Patient Zero, Nathan Bandurski, the first of them to die.

"I don't know what you expect to see that we haven't seen every other time we've looked," Andre said. He was exhausted. Resigned. He looked bad, but he simply refused to give in while there was even a single breath in his lungs, and as far as they could determine Light Sickness wasn't contagious so as long as he could stand he could help.

Sendy would never admit that the real reason he was there was because she was frightened to let him out of her sight.

"I don't know and, honestly, I don't care. I need to be doing something, Andre. I can't just sit on my hands and—" she had been about to say: *wait for you to die.*

She had something she wanted to tell him, something that he needed to know, but not here, not surrounded by the sick and dying. She looked at him. It could wait. She had no idea for how much longer, though.

"Come on, then. Let's do this again." Andre brought up Bandurski's records. The display filled with charts tracking the progression of his illness from the moment he'd collapsed at her feet. His vitals had been weak from the start. His saturation levels too high. But even so, his metabolism burned through the water in his body and started cannibalizing the water in his tissue within hours. That was the crux of it. She thought about the drip-feed pumping hydrogenated solution into his body and how it had barely managed to keep the saturation levels from falling perilously low. Whatever this thing was, it fed on water.

Even in the sickbay Bandurski's condition had quickly worsened, leaving him hovering on the edge of death for days before he finally succumbed.

Andre brought up Vaughan's charts and put them up on the big screen side-by-side. They were depressingly similar and made for grim reading the further down the screen you read. Vaughan was dying. Fast.

"What have we got? What correlation can we see between Bandurski and the rest?"

"Lightspeed," Sendy said. It always came back to that. It was the only common denominator all of the cases shared. They'd been through this a thousand times.

"Lightspeed," Andre agreed. "But what does that *mean*? Are we dying from basically an exaggerated form of travel sickness?"

"I don't know. I don't know. I don't know!" Sendy Montoir railed, frustration getting the better of her. She paced around the cramped medical quarters clenching and unclenching her fists. She swept a burner from the counter top, sending it clattering to the sterile floor.

"But I think I do," he said.

That stopped her dead.

She looked at him, waiting for him to go on, desperate to believe. Desperate to believe he'd solved the riddle and that a cure was there to be manufactured.

He didn't say anything for the longest time, then finally asked, "What did we do?" changing the shape of the question. It was rhetorical this time. "We traveled faster than the speed of light. Think about that for a moment. Faster than the speed of light. Not so long ago lightspeed was the fastest anyone could imagine, wasn't it? There was nothing beyond it. But not anymore." She nodded. They all knew the science of it, and how Chambers-Osawa had undone centuries of scientific belief in one amazing breakthrough. He hadn't just changed the world, he'd changed the building blocks of the universe on them. "What if some things just can't travel that fast? What if we just left something behind?"

"I don't understand what you're saying."

"Bear with me, okay? We've looked at the science from every angle. We've looked at the numbers, the charts, the results, top-to-bottom and bottom-to-top and inside out, and you said it yourself, there's nothing to see. It doesn't matter if they're living or dead, there's nothing to signify why people are getting sick." Andre started to move, becoming more animated with each idea he threw out there until he was matching her pacing. He picked up a reconstructed fruit from the counter and tossed it into the air. The fruit was just one of the many bounties of Sarbras they'd been blessed with. He caught it and then started passing it from hand to hand. "But what if they're not ill at all?" he said at last. "Have you ever considered that? What if that's why we can't find anything? What if it's as simple as some part of us just isn't meant to travel that fast? What if it just can't, or can't keep up, so part of us gets left behind?"

"And that's why the cravings intensify?" Sendy picked up his train of thought. "Is that what you're saying? There's something missing…a gap…and we're gorging on anything and everything that might possibly fill up that emptiness?"

"It's possible."

"Is it?" She asked, skeptically.

"If you think of it from a philosophical standpoint instead of a scientific one, maybe." Andre put the fruit down. Once he had, he didn't seem to know what to do with his hands. She felt sorry for him then. He wanted to crack this thing even more desperately than she did, and not just because of the ticking time bomb his own body had become, but because if the Light Sickness was down to the FTL drives, then he felt responsible. They were his creation. Chambers-Osawa might have hit upon the idea that broke the initial barrier holding them back, but the finished drives were down to Andre Pellar's brilliance. His specifications. His calculations. He had been in that workshop every day, all day and all night. They wouldn't have been built without him. By extension that meant one thousand people wouldn't have been facing an ugly death if it weren't for him. That was the kind of wrong-headed thinking he was torturing himself with. He might not admit it, but she knew him well enough now.

She thought about the whispers she'd heard, about the other appetites on display. "Are you trying to tell me you think the hedonism is down to a desperate need to fill a spiritual void?"

He spread his hands wide. She noticed he was trembling slightly. That was new. He hadn't had tremors before. The sickness was accelerating.

"Maybe it's not just faster than the speed of light," he offered. "I mean, how many times have you heard the expression 'we are beings of light'? Maybe it's faster than the speed of souls? Maybe souls are light?" Andre shrugged, obviously embarrassed by the way his thoughts had turned him from a rational man into a religious absurdist. "It sounds stupid when you say it out loud."

"It does," she agreed. "You're a scientist, not a theologian, Andre."

"I don't know what I am anymore," he admitted. "But it's the only thing that makes sense, even if we don't like the sensing it's making."

She wanted to argue with him. She wanted to point at the fundamental flaw underpinning his argument, but all she could manage was, "We don't even know if souls exist, never mind anything else. How can we build a cure based on nourishing non-existent souls?"

"We can't," Andre admitted. "Maybe there is no cure. Maybe that's what all this means. It's not like we can test the theory. We don't have the wherewithal to recreate the conditions. We can't build new FTL drives. We can't put lab rats into orbit, blast them out for a week-long jump and see if they come back soulless…" Somehow she didn't burst out laughing when he said that, because as ludicrous as it sounded, he was earnest.

"So what can we do?"

"I don't know, but the answer has to be on the *Beacon*. It has to be. Remember, almost everyone I selected for this journey had relatives on the slowship. Genetic relatives. We're all the same, not doppelgängers, but near as damn it. Our genetic codes have the same roots. The fix is there. We just can't see it, but that doesn't mean it isn't there."

"Like God," she said, bitterly. "Seriously, how the hell is that supposed to help? Am I supposed to drag them in here and say, sit down, make yourself comfortable, it's a simple procedure, I just want to do a little soul transfusion, you'll get a free lollipop afterwards if you're brave, I promise."

"I don't know," he admitted, and then he stumbled slightly, reaching out to steady himself. "I haven't thought it through that far. Like you said, I'm not a theologian. If it isn't numbers and formulae I'm lost. Now if there was a way to use numbers to prove the existence of God and souls and all of that stuff, then I'm your man, but until there's an equation for life, I'm useless. If I had to bet my life on it, I still wouldn't know what to say it was." Andre lurched sideways then as his legs gave way beneath him.

Sendy reached out instinctively to catch him, but she couldn't get to Andre before he fell.

He went down hard.

She crouched beside him, cradling his head in her arms. His eyes had rolled up into his skull, showing only jaundiced whites. She smoothed the hair back from his brow. He was burning up beneath her touch.

"Andre! Andre!" she pleaded, trying to bring him round, but he didn't respond.

She picked him up and carried him over to one of the few remaining free beds. They were running out of space in the sickbay, Andre Pellar was running out of time, and Sendy Montoir was running out of ideas.

✦

Andre wore a locket around his neck. It contained a few strands of Renee Sinha's hair. Sendy took it from him and wore it around her own neck, in part because she wanted to be close to anything that was close to him, in part because she wanted to lift the burden it represented from his shoulders. He didn't need the added weight upon his soul.

If he still had one.

✦

The sickbay doors flew open.

A wild-eyed woman stood in the doorway. She looked as though she had run all the way from outpost one, more than a day away. She was breathing hard, her chest heaving beneath her uniform. Sendy Montoir looked at her. Beneath the smears of dirt, grass stains and black smudges she couldn't identify, the woman was familiar. But Sendy was sure they had never met. She would have staked her life on it.

"Can I help you?"

"I had a message to report here urgently. A matter of life and death. I'm Meghan Vaughan."

Vaughan.

It was then that Sendy realized the woman bore a striking resemblance to one of the men in the beds.

"Were you on the *Beacon*?"

"Yes."

"And you received a message from Andre telling you to report here immediately?"

"Sorry?"

"Mr. Pellar summoned you?"

She nodded.

Andre had obviously intended to use her somehow to treat their Vaughan, but how? He hadn't told her half of what was on his mind, and now he wasn't there to ask.

Before she could say anything else a familiar voice crackled across the comms channel, apologizing. It was Andre. She didn't understand how he could be unconscious in the bed and talking to her at the same time, until she realized it wasn't coming from the comms channel at all, it was coming from the sickbay computer, the machine playing back a recording on a loop. The woman's name must have triggered it, she reasoned. Andre must have known there was a chance he wouldn't hold on until she arrived, so when Jorie had requested the latest crew manifests to prepare ballot papers for the election, he had used those few minutes alone to leave her a message. Sendy listened to him now, thinking: *you stupid, stupid, lovely, brilliant man...*

It wasn't quite the same as hearing a voice from beyond the grave, but it was unnerving to hear him repeat his crazy ideas about souls and light and the sucking emptiness of a body without a soul and what that might mean. It sounded like he had given it much more thought than he'd let on before, and he had a scientist's solution...It was quite possibly insane, almost certainly doomed to fail, and Sendy really didn't want to do it. But what if he was right? What if it offered them a chance? What if it could save Andre?

Meghan Vaughan heard everything.

"Will it work?" She asked.

Sendy could have lied to her, but she didn't. "I don't know."

"Are there any alternatives?"

"No."

"Will I die?"

"It's possible," Sendy admitted.

"You're not the best saleswoman," Meghan Vaughan said, and laughed. "Okay, let's do it."

"Are you sure?"

"Not remotely."

✦

Sendy took her under, and side by side with both Vaughans, she ran catheters and drips from her into him and him into her, turning them into an extended system of veins and arteries, merging their bloodstreams. She gave it time for the blood to merge, and then stopped their hearts.

This was the moment of truth.

This was when it could all go so tragically wrong.

She charged the paddles to ten and shocked the woman, bringing her back. Vaughan was harder to resuscitate, but after four jolts, bringing the charge up to eighty, she brought him back, and prayed to whatever god, devil or demon looked after them all that somehow the woman's soul would spill into her blood kin, dividing between them. And if there was no such thing, then she didn't care, just so long as his body fed on hers like a parasite and leeched away whatever nutrient or sustenance it so desperately craved, and brought him back whole. She hoped someone was out there listening.

And then his heart found a rhythm, the beeps on the monitor losing their erratic tachycardia.

The woman came around first, groggy, and with a haunted look behind her eyes. She had just returned from a journey far longer than the trip to Tau Ceti. They didn't talk about it. Sendy brought her a drink, and watched with horror as she guzzled it down greedily, thinking she'd created a second monster rather than saved a sick man. "Thirsty," Meghan Vaughan croaked in a brittle voice. Sendy checked her saturation levels. They were all normal. She was *just* thirsty, Sendy realized. Hoped. It would be weeks before she knew if she was safe from the Light Sickness or if it had become an illness the two Vaughans shared, by which time her Vaughan would be dead again and no amount of electroshock from the crash cart would bring him back.

Four hours later he opened his eyes for the first time in nine days.

There was no way of knowing if it had worked, not yet. There were no tests she could run, no numbers she could count off on a chart. But unlike the others they'd posited, this was an experiment she *could* repeat. Sendy Montoir sent out an urgent summons for any relative of Benitez and Burke to report to the sickbay, and then prepared to kill both of them to save their kin.

She looked at Andre and wondered if she could kill the father of her unborn child, even if it was to save his life?

✦

She went to Jorie Platt's quarters armed with hope.

Jorie could see it on her face the moment she opened the door. She offered Sendy a seat, but she was far too energized to sit still for even a moment. Her children were there, playing noisily. Carrick was in with the Noah making plans for the gradual transplant of the *Beacon*'s indigenous flora and fauna onto Sarbras. It was a huge job. Sendy didn't envy them, but they had prepared all of their lives for it, which was a concept she could barely understand—all of their lives, quite literally. In her world it was the kind of thing you said when you wanted to make an exaggerated point. There was no exaggeration here; the Noah had been born into the role, as had Carrick Platt. This was their reason for living. It went beyond family and love and Jorie herself, and probably Burton and Carrie, into their true purpose.

"Sendy," Jorie said.

"Andre solved it. He found the answer."

"That's brilliant. Fantastic. So how close are you to manufacturing a vaccine?"

"There is no vaccine."

"But I thought…he said that if he could isolate the cause he could work on developing a cure."

"There is a cure. I think."

"A cure but no vaccine? I don't understand."

"Neither do I, really. It's all down to ancestry. Andre worked it out. It's all about faster than light travel, but what he found out was that your passengers are our cure. Every one of us who is related to one of you has a chance. Not a great chance but a chance. But that still means there are two hundred of us without a chance. That's a death sentence for a fifth of our number. And there's not a damned thing we can do for them apart from watch them die."

"Oh god…that's horrible."

"I'm trying not to think about it. I need your crew manifests. I need to compare them with Andre's selection process files, and then start calling people in for treatment."

"Of course. Whatever you need, it's yours."

"Thank you, Jorie. I need to know." This was the one question she hadn't wanted to ask once the solution had started to make itself clear to her. "Did Captain Burton Pellar have any children? Brothers, sisters?"

"Not as far as I know, but I'd need to check ancestral records to see if someone from further down his genetic line, a grandfather's sister, say, married and took a new name. We've got a small gene pool to draw on here, after all, so the chances are good."

"Please do; it's Andre's only chance."

"I'll do it myself, I promise."

Before Sendy could begin to explain the process of the soul transplant, the alarm's claxon blared out through the *Beacon*'s internal speaker system. It was deafening.

Jorie keyed the Bridge on the comms panel and demanded: "This is Platt. Bridge, report. What the hell's happening?"

The voice came back: "Sensors have picked up a ship entering the orbit of Sarbras, Captain. We're not alone."

"What sort of ship?"

"I don't know, Captain, we've never seen anything like it. It came out of nowhere—" which Sendy knew meant it had dropped out of lightspeed.

Jorie turned to Sendy Montoir. "Could Jurudu have sent another ship after you? Even after Andre's transmission? Would he do that?"

"He's not the sort of man who admits defeat," Sendy told her.

They went outside together to watch the skies.

If Jurudu had dispatched another thousand men and women to try and succeed where Vinton had failed he wouldn't have followed the same intense selection process Andre Pellar had, they wouldn't be descendants of the Beacon's first crew up there. They were dead men.

✦

Jurudu looked down on Sarbras.

The *Inquisitor*'s scanners reported life down there: four distinct clusters of it.

FTL travel hadn't torn his body apart. The engines weren't fatally flawed. The ship hadn't broken up under the strain of deceleration. His body hadn't turned to mush. He was here, very much alive.

Pellar had lied to him.

Jurudu felt grim satisfaction at being proved right.

Almost six months without a living soul to interact with had taken its toll on Jurudu. He wasn't the man who had boarded the *Inquisitor*. The solitude had sharpened the edge of madness that had always been present inside him. It had taken longer because the *Inquisitor* had overshot planetfall, and the sub-light drives could only bring her back on course so fast. It meant that he had been out of lightspeed for two whole months by the time he opened up communication channels with Sarbras.

He prepared to broadcast a message down to his people. And they were still his people, no matter what they thought would come of their little treason. A face flickered into view on the screen in front of him. He didn't know the man. It didn't matter.

"This is your President, Elé Jurudu." His voice was brittle from disuse and broke twice in those few words. The man didn't seem to understand him, so Jurudu repeated himself. "I have a message for your command, please see it delivered to your Captain." Another face flicked onto his screen, a woman, quite beautiful if you liked that sort of thing.

"This is Captain Platt," she said.

"Captain. I would speak to the ranking officer from the *Conquistador*."

"You're in no position to make demands, Jurudu. You have no jurisdiction here. This isn't your broken world."

"I am still your President. You are my people. All of you. No matter what stars you walk under. You can't steal what is rightfully mine, but I can share it with you all. I can help you build a perfect world."

"Do you truly believe that? After every atrocity you committed in the name of tomorrow, do you truly believe you can build anything, Jurudu? You're a destroyer. Everything you touch turns to shit. This is our world. It's far from perfect but it's better than anything you ever touched."

"I sent you to this place," Jurudu said, anger surging up inside him. He felt himself getting light-headed with it. Something was wrong. He didn't feel *right*. Nausea threatened to overwhelm him. He needed to be calm. To be reasonable. To lie to them if he had to. It was for the best. "I own you, body and soul," he said, the voice of his madness slipping out between his lips before he could stifle it. "I can forgive you, though, I am a benevolent man. Everything I have ever done has been for the good of my people. But you, you do not understand the full implications of what you have done. You have falsified dispatches, murdered a good man, and despite all that I can forgive your treasons. All I want is the head of the traitor Andre Pellar. In return you can walk at my side into tomorrow. The future is ours, Captain. We can make this world great."

The woman's laughter broke up across the distance.

"You're making threats? You're two days away from landing on the *independent* planet of Sarbras, you're approaching as a hostile and we've got three fully functional plasma cannons down here. Are you really sure you want to do be doing that?" She turned sideways, presenting him with her profile and said something that was lost in a burst of static. A moment later a huge plasma burst lit up the displays, turning pure black space bruise purple.

✦

They looked up at the sky.

They couldn't see Jurudu's ship with the naked eye but they knew it was up there.

"I still don't understand why you didn't just blow him out of the sky," Sendy Montoir said to her friend. "It would have saved so much trouble. He's come out of FTL so he's a dead man walking anyway, you'd be doing him a favor."

"It might start out as that, but where does it end? I don't want to put a single foot on that slippery slope. You don't think Jurudu set out intending to become some despotic lunatic, do you? He was like us once, an idealist with a vision for a better world; you know it and I know it, even if neither of us really wants to think about it."

"But that doesn't change the fact he's still going to cause all sorts of grief before the Light Sickness solves the problem for us."

"All we can do is push through the vote, and face him as a united government, and tell him we don't recognize his authority anymore, we're ceding from the Union of Earth, as simple as that."

Sendy barked out a short laugh. "And you make it sound so easy. I don't suppose a show of hands would do?"

"You know it wouldn't. This has to be done properly or not at all. We only get one shot at democracy. We're either a military hierarchy or we're a government of the people, by the people. We have the time. We can welcome him in style, the first elected government of Sarbras."

Sendy had checked the crew manifests and crosschecked their medical records. One hundred and eighty-seven of the non-ancestral travelers were still alive, but of them more than forty had begun to exhibit the first symptoms of Light Sickness. She couldn't even hope that some few would have a natural immunity because it wasn't an illness, per se. She had yet to tell the unfortunate ones that there was no cure for their condition. Sendy had been putting it off, hoping she'd come up with an alternative, but when Vaughan, Benitez and Burke recovered enough to prove Andre's insane treatment worked, she knew she had no choice but to. Telling Jorie Platt was the first step in forcing herself to face up to her duty as Captain of the *Conquistador*, even though the FTL ship was long since gone.

She handed Jorie the list.

Jorie gave her one in return. It had a single name on it.

"For Andre," she said.

"You found someone?"

Jorie nodded.

Sendy unfolded the paper. She knew the man. Everyone did. It was the Noah.

"He'll never survive the procedure," Sendy said, more hopelessly lost now than ever before.

"He knows that."

"And he's still willing?"

"He's lived a long life. He likes the fact he has a chance to live on in Andre. It's not such a bad way to die, giving the chance of life to someone else. Especially when they're about to become a father for the first time. He's expecting you."

✦

The Noah didn't survive the revival process.

Andre Pellar did.

Barely.

Sendy had done the procedure on more than fifty people now; each time was different, but they always shared the same long moment of doubt when it looked as though they weren't going to come back. Five of them didn't. They died on the table. As she put Andre under, her head swam with so many doubts. She remembered the faces of the ones she'd lost. They were bad enough, but this was worse because this time was the first time she'd had to work on someone she loved.

Watching his heart stop and the monitor flat line she was left in absolutely no doubt that she did love Andre Pellar. Truly. Madly. And with every ounce of her body. There wasn't anything she wouldn't do to bring him back to her. His rhythms peaked, then fell away, peaked then fell away. She gelled up the contact plates on the paddles, charging them to thirty. The jolt of electricity went clean through Andre, causing his body to jerk and spasm in the restraints, but then when the charge was gone, nothing. She did it again, taking it up to fifty. Nothing. Sixty, seventy, eighty, that brutal heartless flat line buzz. Ninety and she was screaming at him to come back to her. One hundred and she knew she'd lost him.

She turned it up to one hundred and sixty. That was far more than the human body was meant to withstand, and as the charge tore through him, Andre's skin blackened across his chest, the paddles branded there like two huge wings over his heart. It worked. She brought him back.

Sendy Montoir collapsed beside the hospital bed. She wept, her tears timed with the steady sinus rhythm of Andre Pellar's beating heart.

She stayed that way for hours.

She never left his side for the nine hours it took for him to open his eyes. When he did, the first thing she said to him was, "Marry me, you crazy, wonderful man."

He said, "Water," and smiled. It was barely a smile. She took it as a yes.

Beside them the Noah lay at peace.

✦

With Jurudu's FTL ship less than a day from landing, Basecamp Hope went to the ballot boxes.

Jorie didn't stand. She had no wish to rule.

It didn't matter. When the ballot papers were counted the overwhelming majority had added her name to the paper. She could have claimed they spoiled the vote, but when all nine thousand votes were tallied (seven thousand from Hope, one thousand from each of the outposts) she had more than eighty-seven percent of the votes. The people had spoken. They wanted Jorie Platt to stay on.

She summoned them to the great hall at the heart of the *Beacon*, with the cargo doors now open onto the lush meadows of Sarbras, and tried to explain why she didn't want to be their President. But before they could misunderstand and think she was throwing their trust back in their faces, Jorie told them: "I am no President. I have no faith in Presidents and no wish to become one. I do not crave the power that comes with the role. I do not need it. Now, admittedly my experience is limited, I have only talked to one of them, but he has proven sadly lacking in, well, in almost every area, but mostly in terms of sanity. Even now his craft approaches. He is alone. He is coming single-handedly to claim our world and us for his own. I will not allow that, but neither will I be your President. Frankly, I would rather chew through my own arm, before I donned that mantle...*But* I would be honored to maintain the rank of Captain and help however I can so that all of us can find a better life planet-side."

She looked out across the sea of faces. The fact that she was accepting their confidence finally sank in. When it did, the first voice went up: "Long live Captain Platt!" Others took up the cry. And so it was that the last Captain of the *Beacon* became the first Captain of Basecamp Hope.

✦

Jurudu was no fool. He knew he couldn't fight them single-handedly, but he had no choice but to try and bluster and hope that they would accept they had done wrong. He knew, even as he began to walk down the ramp onto the surface of Sarbras, that there would be no such reversal. A thousand of these people had only left Earth less than a year ago. These really were his people, not the traitor's spawn from the *Beacon*. He needed to appeal to them, and for that he needed to appear strong. But as another wave of sickness churned within his gut and his balance threatened to betray him he felt anything but.

He refused to believe that Pellar hadn't been lying. The man was a duplicitous piece of shit. He couldn't tell the truth if it ran up to him and took a huge chunk of meat out of his flabby backside. The pair of them were strangers.

Jurudu stumbled but he did not fall.

The timing of it could not have been worse. He looked up as he steadied himself to see his welcoming committee, and in the middle of them, pale-faced and sickly, was the traitor himself. To the others it would have looked as though he'd seen Pellar and his legs buckled. Behind the traitor the flag flew over the basecamp. Jurudu thought at first it was his seal in the center of the flag but it wasn't. As the breeze picked up, the flag unfurled to reveal the star of Tau Ceti in its place. He stiffened, biting down on the urge to yell, "This is my world!" Appearances were important and Jurudu despised weakness. Equally he had no time for petulance or pedantry. He needed to show these ingrates how strong he really was, and the first stage in that would be dealing with the traitor. He locked eyes with Pellar.

"You are a dead man," Jurudu said, calmly. There was no anger or vitriol in his voice, but it was still weak. The words carried.

"That is more true than you could possibly know," Andre Pellar said.

He addressed Pellar, but in truth he was talking to the entire crew of the *Conquistador*. "You lied to me, Pellar. You lied to our entire world. We gave you everything you needed for this incredible journey, we sent you on your way. Every last man and woman from the *Conquistador*, we sent you on your way with our hope for the future in your hands, and you betray us like this?" He spread his arms wide, to take it all in. "We should have been able to share in your triumph. You should have become a beacon of hope to everyone you left behind, but Pellar sent back pictures of a burning world and snatched that last hope from the world. You haven't just betrayed me with your lies, you have turned your back on the poor, the hungry, you have turned your back on the weak and the defenseless, the desperate. You've turned your back on your own families and loved ones that didn't make this journey with you. You've lied to them all and snatched any kind of hope from them, leaving them on a dying world while you live in the land of plenty. How did you sink so low? How could you hate them so much? I don't understand. Tell me. Make me see." Jurudu was leaning heavily on the ship's guardrail before he finished. The ground threatened to lurch out from under him.

No one moved to help him. He would have refused their help if they had.

"So I lied to you?" Pellar admitted. "I did it for eight thousand people and the thousands upon thousands before them who had set out on the greatest pilgrimage of our world, and I did it for Renee Sinha. I saw what your goons did to her, Jurudu. I saw everything when you opened the data files to me. I saw it all. All of the people your regime tortured in your name, all the dissidents who dared to speak out against you, I saw how you made them disappear. So I made us disappear. I didn't want you sending an invasion fleet after us. I knew you would. I'd seen the plans for the *Inquisitor* Class fleet. I needed something that would keep you away."

"You murdered Karl Vinton."

It wasn't Pellar that replied, it was a woman. He recognized her vaguely. She was part of Vinton's crew. She stood beside the traitor so he knew he could not trust a word that came out of her mouth. "Vinton suffered a seizure before he could be tried for his crimes."

Jurudu grunted.

"I am supposed to believe that he simply had a heart attack out of what, guilt? Do I look like I was born yesterday? What you did was mutinous, soldier. You killed the Captain of a Union of Earth ship. That is a court-martialing offense."

She didn't rise to the bait.

He wanted to goad them into saying something he could use to turn the others to his side. There was a balance here, between old loyalties and new, and in some of the listeners it was precarious at best. Others were just waiting for an excuse to side with him, because they'd never really broken their ties with Earth and he was still their rightful ruler.

Jurudu had a splitting headache.

Pellar saw him wince.

He cursed his own damned body.

"You're dying, Jurudu. Can't you feel it? I might have been lying but I wasn't wrong. Faster-than-light travel is a killer. It's eating away at you. By the looks of your body you haven't got long left. I've brought some people to meet you. I want them to tell you in their own words what happened to them after they arrived here. You don't have to believe me, but these people have nothing to gain from lying to you. We call it Light Sickness. It affects people at different rates, but every single one of us who traveled on the *Conquistador* has been infected. There's no conventional cure. No pill or vaccine. And if you don't have genetic relatives that traveled on the slow-ship, there's nothing we can do. Tell me, are you hungry yet? Thirsty?"

He was ravenous, he realized. He couldn't remember the last time he had eaten. He was finding it harder and harder to think straight. They were trying to trick him with their clever words and promises of death. They had drugged him, somehow, targeted him with some form of hallucinogenic, something. They must have done something. He would not be tricked into submission. His soldiers were scattered throughout the crowd. He would order them to rise up in his name. He would order them to bring down this false leadership and restore the flag of Earth and he would have the head of Andre Pellar and the mutinous woman on spikes before the day was done.

"I am President Elé Jurudu, democratically elected ruler of the Earth. You might fly a new flag but you are still my people. Mark my words well: I do not recognize your authority to secede from my rule. That means that any of you who do not bow the knee to me now will be deemed traitors, found guilty of treason, and treason is punishable by death. I have no wish to shed blood. Any who bow down to me will be forgiven. You have my word."

✦

And some did bow down to him, metaphorically if not physically. There were plenty of people angry enough at the injustice of their lives being ended by the journey to Sarbras, and bitter that they had no blood relatives on the slowship that could save them. They didn't have time to speak out.

Jurudu fell before he set foot on Sarbras.

He sagged and stumbled and fell, rolling down the ramp. He was unconscious as he sprawled across the dirt, truly making planetfall.

Sendy Montoir and three of her sickbay team carried the fallen President into Basecamp Hope. They cared for him despite the fact that personally she wanted to leave him out there to rot. Sendy was savvy, she knew full well that there were still people who felt they owed some sort of loyalty to the old world. She knew she had to tread softly around them and be seen to do everything properly. Their newly elected democracy was less than a day old. How it dealt with the ex-iled dictator would speak volumes for the integrity of it. She had no doubt that in their place Jurudu would have ignored any sort of protocol and would have had no time for niceties. They were a threat to the peace, and there would have been an unfortunate accident waiting to befall them in their sleep. It was as simple as that. Men like Jurudu dealt with problems ruthlessly.

As much as it pained her, she agreed with Andre. They couldn't stoop to his level. They had left that world of torturers and lies behind. As much as he hated Karl Vinton and by extension his master, the man who had turned a blind eye to Vinton's ruthless excess, Andre was not him and would not become him. She loved him all the more for it, but was quite happy to do the dirty work on his behalf. She didn't tell him that.

Sendy didn't leave the dictator's sickbed even for an hour. She couldn't risk someone coming in looking to ensure he didn't wake up. The man was dying; they didn't need to hurry it along. His death was never going to be simple. Andre joined her death watch, sitting in a chair beside Jurudu's bed. He was still too weak to really help, but his mind was as sharp as ever and despite Jurudu's order Andre refused to just let him die. He asked Sendy to run blood spinal fluid tests on the man, and then pleaded with Jorie Platt to run the results against the DNA banks they'd built over the last month or so cataloguing the genetic heritage of every single traveler. He'd never expected to find a match but he should have known he would. Fate was cruel like that.

The hit came back positive. Jurudu had a familial bond with one man from the *Beacon*. Andre took no pleasure in telling Jorie Platt that the love of her life was blood kin to the dictator. The genetic markers indicated a close bond. A perfect match.

He left them to think about the implications of the match.

In a brief moment of lucidity Sendy sat down with Jurudu and tried once more to explain as best she could the soul transplant procedure. Sweat matting his hair to his feverish brow, Jurudu looked at her as though she were the Devil herself.

"I am not having the blood of some traitor flowing through my veins, woman, and you are a damned fool for even suggesting it. I am Jurudu. I would rather die than let such impurity into my body. I don't know how you did it, but I know you are behind this sickness. I know that it is some kind of trick. I will not give you the satisfaction of polluting my flesh with your traitor's spirit."

"It's your only chance," Sendy said yet again, tired of arguing the same point with him over and over again. He sapped her strength. He was barely coherent most of the time now, and even when he was he was tormented by paranoid delusions. He saw enemies in every shadow, and plots knotting all around him.

His musculature withered, but he ignored it stubbornly. He must have been tormented by the same hungers that tore at the other victims of Light Sickness but the sheer strength of Jurudu's will meant he refused to surrender to those cravings, thinking he could beat them. And perhaps he could. Perhaps he would prove to be naturally immune—*after all*, Sendy thought, *he hadn't had a soul to start with*. Even so, the appetites tormented him to the point of rabidity, but so long spent alone in course-correction, approach and then orbit and landing had damaged Jurudu in ways that other victims of Light Sickness hadn't been affected.

✦

Jurudu knew he was dying. He wasn't stupid. And, in retrospect, given the choice of this death or the one Juno Lynn had offered, he would have taken Lynn's every time of asking. Carrick Platt was his only hope. That was no hope at all. He would not let them operate on him.

Instead, he told Pellar and Platt and Montoir, alone and together, that he did not recognize their authority, that this damned insurrection was unlawful and that each and every last one of them would hang for what they had done to him. He wanted them to kill him. If they wouldn't, then he would have to take it out of their hands. If he could kill all of them, then so much the better.

When, finally, driven beyond the point of exhaustion Sendy Montoir fell asleep at his bedside, Elé Jurudu summoned one last colossal effort from his weakened body and crawled on his hands and knees to the sickbay's command console, intent on sending out one last defiant message urging those still loyal to him to rise up.

He placed his hand flat on the console, unsure whether the machine would recognize him. It wasn't the *Inquisitor* or the *Conquistador*, after all. This shipboard computer had been installed almost two hundred years before he had been born. It didn't recognize him. Refusing to be thwarted by something so simple, Jurudu crossed the sickbay to the mortuary drawers and hauled open one of them. He used the dead man's hand to initiate comms.

"Hear me, my people," he said, leaning close to the console because his voice didn't have the strength to carry. His words went out to every corner of the old slowship, waking every sleeper. "This is Elé Jurudu, your rightful ruler. They have poisoned me. I am dying. They pretend to care for me but they are merely monitoring my death. It is the same for you they have damned two hundred of you, and claim it is because you have no soul, but ask yourself this, isn't it more reasonable to believe that it is because they believe you are a threat to their new world? They scheme and lie behind your backs picking who will live and who will die. Well, I say to you, my people, those they would simply leave to die, rise up. Rise up. Save yourselves! Rise up!"

And then the loyal few started hammering at the sickbay doors.

✦

Carrick Platt was a good man. That was what killed him.

Woken by Jurudu's broadcast, he knew his wife would need him. He made sure the children were safe first, and told them not to open the door for anyone, then went in search of Jorie, knowing she would be in the thick of it.

He rushed through the old corridors of Basecamp Hope. He knew them like the back of his hand. He must have walked this stretch between their quarters and the Eden Atrium ten thousand times. More. But this was unlike any of those other times. Claxons blared out their deafening warnings, cycling madly louder and louder as the confines of the old slowship came under threat. He could feel the blows pounding through the metal floor beneath his feet and shivering through the walls and ceiling all around him.

They were turning on each other. Fear did that to them. Fear that Jurudu brought with them. Before his arrival they had faced every threat together, even when it seemed like there was no hope for some of them, they hadn't abandoned each other. But Jurudu had driven a wedge between them with a few emotive words. It was as simple as that. No amount of external threat could have been as divisive as Jurudu's assertion that they weren't all equals in this new world.

Carrick Platt had never hated anyone before in his life. He had been raised amid the flora and fauna that the slowship had brought with it from the old Earth, and was more at home with plants than people. He understood the hierarchy of animals, though, and how Jurudu had opened up a wound that doubt and fear and anger at the unjustness of their impending deaths swelled in to fill. The two hundred crew members of the *Conquistador* who didn't have blood kin on the slowship were like wounded animals, cornered, frightened, desperate and lashing out. More than anything they just wanted to know they still had a chance. They were living out their last days in a place called Hope, they deserved that much at least. He wished he could give it to them. He couldn't. The only person he could help was the man who had set this chain of events into motion. Jurudu. The first man he had ever hated. The irony of it did not escape Carrick Platt.

In the distance he heard the clash of factions coming together. The hysteria of raised voices. The screams of battle and pain. They spiraled out of control. The roar of violence charged down the corridors. The thunder of fists and pipes and any other makeshift weapon that could be brought to hand hammered against the very fabric of the old ship. It made Carrick's head spin.

He needed to get to his wife's side.

He needed to be with her.

But he didn't know where she would be in all of this.

Two hundred against almost seven thousand wouldn't, under normal circumstances, have been much of a fight. But these were anything but normal circumstances. The two hundred men were gripped by the frenzy of excess that Light Sickness brought with it, and as the adrenaline surged through their system it only served to turn them rabid. There was no calming them. They would simply burn out when their bodies lost the strength to fight on. Until then they were on a blood high.

Carrick ran hard, arms and legs pumping furiously as he turned the corner toward the command block and the Bridge, thinking Jorie might be trapped there. In front of him twenty blood-matted men in the torn rags of their uniforms battered on the sealed doors. The doors would never yield but that didn't deter them. Their bloodied knuckles dragged either on the floor or across the walls as they turned one after the other to see Carrick at the other end of the corridor. They shuffled forward a step, and then another. Nostrils flared, lips curled back baring teeth streaked with blood.

Carrick had never seen anything like it in his life.

He couldn't move.

There was a moment when it seemed the rioters would lose interest in him and turn back to the door and continue their hopeless quest to break on through to the other side, but one of them pointed at him and it was as though all of the others shared some telepathic connection and just simply understood that unlike the door he *would* yield. They came for him.

Carrick ran, but he didn't stand a chance.

✦

Jurudu ran with the mob.

He felt more alive than he had felt in years.

It was the last rally of the flesh before it succumbed to death. He knew that. He had come to understand his body. He could thank the traitors for that, he supposed. Whatever they had done to him, it had worked. He wouldn't see the coming dawn. He wouldn't stand triumphant in the great hall of the slowship and claim his right as President to rule them, putting the upstarts in their place. His muscles were wasted to the point he could only run a dozen steps before he had to reach out for support as his legs buckled. He was like some newborn buck barely able to stagger a few steps at a time. But he would be damned if he was simply going to lie in that sickbed and wait for death.

Jurudu wanted one thing before he died: the head of Andre Pellar.

It wasn't a lot to ask out of life.

He broke away from the mob to go hunting.

✦

Andre found Carrick Platt in the corridor outside the Bridge, bleeding out.

He had a pulse, but it was desperately weak and erratic. Judging by the huge pool of blood he lay in, Carrick had lost far too much blood for his system not to crash. Andre wasn't a medic, but even he could see that.

"Stay with me," he urged. "Just let me get you to the medics. Please." Still weak from the after effects of Light Sickness, Andre gathered Carrick up into his arms. He was distressingly light. Andre carried his friend toward the sickbay.

He could hear sounds of violent clashes in the distance.

Jorie had dispatched containment crews.

The fighting wouldn't last long now.

But, he realized, as the sounds of fighting grew closer with each step, the worst of it was in between him and the sickbay.

The old slowship was a maze. There were a dozen other corridors he could take to reach the sickbay, but this was the most direct route, and Carrick didn't have long. And he wasn't strong enough to go looking for an alternate passage.

✦

Jurudu saw him.

✦

Andre Pellar saw Jurudu.

They faced each other like gunslingers down the long corridor. There was no one else between them. The sickbay was no more than one hundred yards beyond him but it might as well have been one hundred light years.

"He needs help," Andre said, trying to reason with him.

"I don't care about him," Jurudu said matter-of-factly. "It's you I want to kill, Traitor."

"Just let me get him to the sickbay then you can kill me."

"No."

And so saying, Jurudu started to run at him, hands outstretched as though he intended to throttle the life out of Andre. Andre barely had time to put Carrick Platt down before the mad Jurudu was on him and they were locked in a deadly embrace. Jurudu's big murderous hands closed around his throat, his thumbs pressing at his Adam's Apple. Andre couldn't break the hold. He choked, gasping for breath. He clawed at Jurudu's hands as they twisted and staggered, locked in their deadly dance. And then something inside Andre Pellar snapped. And whatever that something was, it had been holding back Renee Sinha's ghost. He saw her. He heard her. It was like she had never gone. *But she is gone*, he realized, flapping at Jurudu's face. His vision swam as he danced right along the edge of unconsciousness. And then the thought blazed across his mind: *he took her from me*. In that moment it didn't matter that he had found happiness again, that was neither here nor there. This man had let that monster Vinton brutalize the woman he loved. He had the chance to put it right. It wasn't revenge. It was justice. He had killed Vinton, and now he would kill Jurudu, this time with his bare hands.

Andre Pellar's hands closed around Jurudu's throat and he choked the life out of the man who once upon a time had ruled the world.

✦

Andre carried Carrick into the sickbay.

"Oh, my god," Sendy gasped, seeing them. "Is he?" She couldn't bring herself to say the word dead.

"Almost."

"Put him on the bed, quickly. We need a medic. Not me. I can't do this."

"Yes you can," Andre said calmly. "You're his only chance."

Sendy didn't argue. She checked his wounds. He had several that needed sealing and suturing. One pierced his liver. Another seemed to have damaged his kidneys. He had taken a hell of a beating. He had no right to still be alive.

He wouldn't be for much longer.

"I can't do this. He's dead, Andre. His kidneys, his liver, his entire body is shutting down. The damage is massive. He's hemorrhaging internally. Without transfusions, organ transplants—"

"There are new organs, everything you need. Fresh. Less than two minutes dead."

She didn't understand what he was saying.

"Jurudu," Andre said. "He wouldn't let Carrick save his life, now the bastard is going to save Carrick's. Call it poetic justice."

Andre went back to fetch the President's corpse.

4

221 years since the Beacon's *departure from Earth.*
Year Four: Tau Ceti.

THE TWINS WERE PLAYING on the lawn with Burton and Carrie. Andre and Sendy sat side-by-side, inseparable. The sun was up and it was a beautiful day. Every day was a beautiful day now. She saw Jorie and Carrick walking back from the wall of remembrance with young Jurudu swinging between them. She hadn't liked the idea of that name living on, but couldn't argue with Carrick's logic. Without him Carrick would have died, and parts of his blood kin lived on inside him even now. The wall of remembrance listed the name of every man, woman and child that had made the journey from Earth whether they had reached Tau Ceti or not.

The girls saw young Jurudu and went racing toward him, squealing and laughing as they vied for his attention. In twenty years there would be hearts broken, but today there was nothing more at risk than a few grass stains.

Sendy Pellar took her husband's hand in hers.

"There's something I need to tell you," she said. She had rehearsed the speech in her head over and over a hundred times.

"You can tell me anything."

"Promise?"

"You know I do. What's on your mind, love?"

"I wanted to give you something…"

"You've already given me the world and then some, Sendy," Andre said. "You know that. Before you I was nothing."

"That's not true, Andre. You were always you. I'm pregnant again." His face lit up. That smile of his always broke her heart, it was just so full of kindness and love. She touched a finger to his lips before he could interrupt her. She needed to get this out, to explain. "It's another girl." He grinned lopsidedly at that. "But she's not *just* ours." She took Renee Sinha's locket out of her pocket, wondering if he would understand what she had done. "There were still follicles attached to the roots of Renee's hair. I had one of the techs in the birthing chamber encode her DNA on my egg. This baby girl I am carrying is mine, yours and Renee's. I owe her every moment of my happiness. It's hard to explain. I wanted to give her back to you, Andre, but not as some ghost I could never compete with. I wanted to give her a place in this future, because without her none of us would have one."

"Can I kiss you now?"

♈

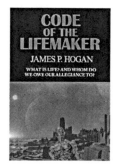

CPSIA information can be obtained at www.ICGtesting.com
Printed in the USA
BVOW040540160513

320835BV00001B/1/P